WE WERE THERE

At the First
Airplane Flight

"The birds have the secret," Orville said to Wilbur

WE WERE THERE

At the First
Airplane Flight

Felix Sutton

Illustrated by
Laszlo Matulay

Dover Publications, Inc.
Mineola, New York

To the Memory of
Weyman Coe
A Pioneer of the Air

Bibliographical Note

This Dover edition, first published in 2013, is an unabridged republication of the work originally published in 1960 by Grosset & Dunlap, New York.

Library of Congress Cataloging-in-Publication Data

Sutton, Felix.

We were there at the first airplane flight / Felix Sutton; illustrated by Laszlo Matulay.

p. cm.

"This Dover edition, first published in 2013 is an unabridged republication of the work originally published in 1960 by Grosset & Dunlap, New York."

Summary: "On a blustery North Carolina afternoon in 1902, young Jimmie and Clara Blair meet Orville and Wilbur Wright and assist the inventors in realizing their dream of human flight"— Provided by publisher.

ISBN-13: 978-0-486-49258-2 (pbk.)

ISBN-10: 0-486-49258-3

1. Wright, Orville, 1871–1948—Juvenile fiction. 2. Wright, Wilbur, 1867–1912—Juvenile fiction. [1. Wright, Orville, 1871–1948—Fiction. 2. Wright, Wilbur, 1867–1912—Fiction. 3. Flight—History—Fiction. 4. Airplanes—History—Fiction. 5. Inventors—Fiction.] I. Matulay, Laszlo, illustrator. II. Title.

PZ7.S9682Wh 2013
[Fic]—dc23

2013018747

Manufactured in the United States by Courier Corporation
49258302   2014
www.doverpublications.com

Contents

Illustrations

WE WERE THERE

At the First
Airplane Flight

This Saturday, Jimmy thought, was perfect kite weather

CHAPTER ONE

The Kite Fliers

1902

THE east wind, blowing in strong, steady gusts from the choppy waters of the Atlantic, whistled over the high sand dunes of the Kitty Hawk peninsula and swirled skyward in powerful, sweeping updrafts. Flocks of sea gulls, their wings rigid and motionless, rode these uprushing columns of air into the clear blue sky. They soared in wide lazy circles until they were almost out of sight.

This Saturday afternoon, Jimmy Blair thought, was perfect for flying a kite. But then just about any day was perfect kite weather on this long, narrow finger of sand that lay off the coast of North Carolina between the ocean and Albemarle Bay.

Right at the moment, though, Jimmy had his hands full. It was all he could do to keep the stiff wind from snatching his big kite off the ground before he was ready to launch it. He was trying to hold the kite down with one hand while he fastened a heavy fishline to it with the other.

For most of his fifteen years, Jimmy had been building and flying kites. He'd started out making kites in the standard pattern of the day—two crossed sticks covered with old newspapers and held together by a thick paste of flour and water. Then he had gradually branched out with novel designs of his own.

Some of these Jimmy Blair originals had flown, but most of them had smashed into the ground the instant the treacherous wind currents of Kitty Hawk hit them. But Jimmy had never given up trying. And this newest kite which he was about to launch was the most unusual he had ever built.

He'd copied its design from a picture in *Scientific American* of a glider in which a man named Otto Lilienthal, over in Germany, had actually soared for short distances through the air. It consisted of two bat-like wings, made of split bamboo ribs covered with light silk, and held together by bamboo struts. The effect was like that of a box kite that had only the top and bottom sides covered. Jimmy didn't quite see what would hold it steady in the air. But if the German could make a contraption like this fly, maybe he could too.

As he struggled to tie the line to the two end struts of the kite, the wind whipped the silk covering so hard that Jimmy was afraid it was going to rip clean off. He sure wished Clara would hurry up and get here. It was going to take both of them to get this kite into the air today.

Kneeling on one knee, holding the kite down firmly on the sand, he glanced upward at the circling gulls.

Now there, he thought, was the perfect flying machine. Wings straight out and rigid, body neatly balanced in between them. He had read somewhere that birds could fly because their feathers were so light. But he knew this was a crazy idea. A feather would fall to the ground just like anything else. Besides, he had shot a grouse last fall on his grandfather's farm over beyond Elizabeth City. And when he had picked up the big bird, which had been so graceful and weightless in the air a few minutes before, it was as heavy as a two-pound piece of steak.

No, it wasn't a bird's feathers that held it up. It was the way their wings and their bodies were put together. If somebody could only get close enough to a soaring gull to see how its wings worked, maybe he'd find the answer to heavier-than-air flight. But meanwhile, people would just have to go along blindly experimenting with things like this kite he was holding.

As these thoughts ambled through Jimmy's mind, he heard a shout. A girl in a blue dress appeared over the top of the dune, her bright red hair flying in the breeze.

"Well, thunderation, Clara!" Jimmy said impatiently. "Did you come by way of Raleigh? You know I can't get this kite into the air unless you hold it for me. And the wind has like to torn the covering off it while I've been here waiting."

"I'm sorry, Jimmy," the girl said. "I had to run an errand for Mama. But I came as soon as I could."

Clara Blair was a year younger than her brother, and like Jimmy she was tall and thin. But there the resemblance ended. Jimmy's skin was burned a deep tan by the Carolina sun and wind, in sharp contrast to his yellow hair. Clara's face was a mass of freckles under long curls the brilliant scarlet of a southern sunset.

Jimmy stood up and handed the kite to his sister. Then he picked up the reel of stout fishline.

"Now hold it steady by these two struts," he instructed, "while I walk the line down to the bottom of the hill. I'll yell: 'One—two—three—*go!*' And when I say, '*Go,*' just let it loose. Don't push it or shove it. Just let go of it. I'll do the rest."

Jimmy backed down the sand-hill, paying out the line from his reel. At the bottom, he tightened the line until it stretched taut from his hand to the kite. He waited a minute or two until he could feel a fresh gust of wind blowing steadily on his back. Then he sang out:

"All right! One—two—three—*go!*"

At the word *Go!* Clara released the kite, and Jimmy pulled hard on the line. The wind, rushing up the side of the slope, caught the silk-covered wings and shot the kite straight into the air. The line sang as it peeled off the spinning reel, and the kite fought it like a bucking bronco, jerking and kicking as though trying to shake off the slender thread that bound it to the earth.

Jimmy snubbed the whistling line in an effort to get the kite under better control, releasing it slowly as the kite tugged and pulled. Up, up, up it went until nearly all of the two hundred feet of line had spun off the reel. Then, very carefully, he began to wind it in.

Jimmy's heart was pounding so hard that it made an ache in his throat as he watched this new kite of his ride the wild currents of the wind. Boy, oh boy! he thought. He'd never built anything like this one before! But this sure was the way to do it! The German, Lilienthal, was right! Built a kite, or a glider, with two wings, one on top of the other! Why, gosh! If you made a kite about four times as big as this one, a man could lie stretched out on the lower wing, and . . .

Without warning, the shifting wind blew the daydream abruptly out of his head. The kite bucked heavily, fell off on one wing-tip, and shot straight down like a lead weight. Frantically, Jimmy reeled in his line, running backwards as he did so. But nothing he could do was able to get the kite back on an even keel or halt its suicidal plunge to the ground.

Clara shrieked: "Oh-h!" And an instant later the kite slammed heavily onto the the hard-packed sand and crumpled into a shapeless mass of silk and bamboo.

It had all happened so suddenly that Jimmy could hardly believe it. One second he was picturing himself riding serenely on the kite's lower wing; and the next second—

Gosh all hemlock! Suppose he *had* been riding it! He blew out a deep breath and wiped a bead of cold sweat from his forehead.

"Oh, golly, Jim!" Clara said sympathetically. "Your beautiful kite! Did I do anything wrong?"

Jimmy's heart, which was so high a few seconds

before, had hit the bottom of his stomach with a thud he could almost hear. But he tried to act as though mishaps like this were all in a day's work for scientific experimenters. He picked up the shattered remains of the kite and looked at them for a long moment.

"Oh, well! Twenty-three skidoo!" he said, and tossed the fragments into the air. A gust of wind caught them and whisked them out of sight.

"Of course you didn't do anything wrong," he said in answer to Clara's anxious question. "She went up just dandy. But once she caught a cross-current of wind, she couldn't adjust herself to it."

"Maybe it needs a tail," Clara suggested. She'd been helping her brother for years, and as a result she knew more about kites than any boy she knew except Jimmy.

"No-o," Jimmy said thoughtfully. "With this kind of a kite, a tail hanging down would only get in the way."

He looked up again at the soaring gulls, effortlessly riding the same veering winds that had sent his kite plunging to destruction.

"Gulls don't have tails," he mused, half aloud. "Leastwise, not tails like the ones on kites. But look how they coast on the wind. When it changes, they change with it. Maybe if I covered a kite with feathers, the wind would get in between them so that every feather would act as a lifting surface. Then the air currents might swing the wings around and keep them always headed into the wind. Hmmm! By jiminy, you know, Clara, that just might be the—"

Suddenly Clara gasped, and grasped his arm.

"J-Jimmy!" she stuttered, pointing to the sky behind him. "Oh, great day, Jimmy! Look!"

Jimmy lazily looked around, and then his mouth popped open in wonderment.

"Ho-ly mo-ly!" he whispered, hardly able to credit what his eyes were seeing. "Hul-ly gee!"

He jumped to his feet and stood staring, speechless, at a strange apparition that hung in the sky over Kill Devil Hill, five hundred feet away.

It was a kite, very much like the one he had been trying to fly, but of gigantic size. Like his kite, it had an upper and a lower wing, held together by struts. But while the wing-spread of his kite had only been two feet, this monster was close to thirty.

It had a third small wing jutting out in front, and a high, thin rudder in the back. Two long, thin skids, like sled runners, extended from front to back under the bottom wing. Rope lines trailed down from each wing-tip, obviously being held by men who were out of sight on the far side of the dune.

After the first few startled moments, Jimmy found his voice:

"My land, Clara, will you look at that! And you see those little rudder things? They're the secret! They're what keep her steady in the wind!"

He started to run across the sand.

"Come on," he shouted over his shoulder. "I've got to see what's going on."

Jimmy breasted the sand hill with Clara close at his heels. In the little valley beyond the dune, he could see two men—one very tall and thin, and the other just as thin but not quite so tall—holding the two lines that tethered the monster kite.

As he watched, the big kite dipped suddenly, just as his had done a few minutes before, and started to hurl itself at the ground.

"Quick, Orv!" the tall man yelled. "Straighten her up!"

The other hauled mightily on his line, and the kite momentarily came back to level flight. Then another swift gust of wind hit it and drove it into the sand. The forward rudder crumpled on the impact.

"Oh, thunder!" the tall man said angrily. "There goes another two days' work. We've got to do something about those wings, Orv. But I'll be jiggered if I know what."

The two men were fighting to keep the broken kite from being blown away by the high wind when Jimmy and Clara approached them.

"Can I give you a hand, mister?" Jimmy asked. The tall man looked up.

"Thanks," he said. "We could use it. This wind's rough today. If you'll lift up the tail, son, I'll take this wing, and Orv can carry the other. Our camp's just a little way beyond that dune."

As the three of them carried the giant kite, or glider, or whatever it was, over the rolling dunes, with Clara bringing up the rear, Jimmy examined it closely. The wings were made of a light, muslin-like fabric stretched over curved ribs that caused the wings to be thicker in the middle than they were at either edge. The tail rudder, which Jimmy was holding, was a thin, rigid cloth-covered frame-work of wood.

The younger man, the one called Orv, spoke to Jimmy over his shoulder as they walked along.

"Young fellow, was that your little glider that went up a moment ago over yonder?"

Jimmy nodded and grinned sheepishly.

"Yes, sir. But I'm afraid she came down a whole lot faster than she went up."

"I didn't know anybody down in this part of the country was interested in flying machines. Where did you get the idea for the biplane design?"

Jimmy wrinkled his forehead.

"The *what-kind-of* design?"

Orv laughed. "The double wings."

"Oh," Jimmy said. Then he told him about the picture in *Scientific American*. "I've been fooling around with kites ever since I was big enough to fly one."

"So have we. And some people back home in Dayton, Ohio, think we're a little bit crazy. But someday, somebody is going to build a flying machine that will really fly, and we think we're on the right track."

Jimmy had read everything he could get his hands on about the flying machine experiments of Professor Langley and Dr. Alexander Graham Bell and Sir Hiram Maxim, but he'd never dreamed that he might actually meet up with real, live flying machine inventors. He wondered who these fellows were. They looked mighty young to be scientists.

As if reading his thoughts, the younger of the two men said:

"By the way, my name is Orville Wright. And this is my brother Wilbur."

CHAPTER TWO

The Inventors

CARRYING the glider easily between them—
for all its size, Jimmy figured, it couldn't have
weighed more than a hundred pounds—he and
the Wrights rounded the base of the big sand dune
called Kill Devil Hill, and came to the inventors'
camp. It consisted of a large wooden shack and a
smaller canvas tent.

The front wall of the shack was hinged at the
top, so that when it was lifted and propped up by
poles at each corner, it made a sort of roofed front
porch. Inside, the shack was empty except for a
long workbench that ran along one wall, two rum-
pled cots, an alcohol stove, a plain deal dining
table, and a few canvas chairs. They carried the
glider through the front opening and put it on the
floor beside the rear wall.

"What did you say your name was, son?"
Wilbur Wright, the older brother, asked.

"Jimmy Blair, sir. I live over in Nag's Head."

"Well, thanks, Jimmy. You've been a big help."
He fished into his trouser pocket. "Here's a dime
for your trouble."

Jimmy didn't want to take the money, but he
was afraid Mr. Wright would think him impolite
if he refused. So he mumbled his thanks.

"Say, Orv," Wilbur said. "Run out and draw us
a pail of water, will you? I want to get busy on this
rudder while it's still light enough to see."

Jimmy jumped for the water bucket on the floor
beside the stove.

"I'll get it, sir," he said. He went outside, filled the bucket at a pitcher pump perched on the top of a length of pipe that was stuck into the sand, and carried it back in.

"Is—is there anything else I can do for you, Mr. Wright?" he asked hesitantly. He was desperately trying to find an excuse to stay here in this exciting place where grown men flew kites that were thirty feet wide and talked about someday building a flying machine that would really fly. "Can I gather you up some—some firewood or something?"

Wilbur looked thoughtful for a moment as he scratched his long, bony chin.

"Jimmy," he said, nodding his head, "I think maybe you showed up at a good time. We hired an old man to run errands for us and help around the camp; but his feet hurt all the time and his rheumatism bothered him, and so yesterday morning he quit. How would you like his job?"

Jimmy's face lit up like one of those new-fangled electric lights.

"Gee, Mr. Wright! I'd like that fine. I have to be in school every week day till two-thirty, but I could be here by three and get all the chores done before dark. And I could work all day Saturdays and Sundays."

"Okay," Wilbur said. "You're hired. The pay will be three dollars a week."

Jimmy was breathless. Boy! Things sure had been happening thick and fast today!

"I don't want any money," he said quickly. He didn't know how to explain that watching the brothers work on their glider, and fly it, would be pay enough.

Wilbur shook his head.

"No. A good day's work is always worth a good day's pay. Besides," he grinned, "if we weren't paying you, we couldn't bawl you out when you fell down on the job. So your pay will be three dollars a week, cash on the barrelhead every Saturday. Now run out to the supply tent and bring in a couple of cans of beans and a side of bacon. It's Orv's turn to be cook tonight."

Clara had been standing outside the shack, cautiously peering in through the wide door. In there was a man's world, a world in which she had no part, and it made her uneasy. As Jimmy dashed past her on his way to get the supplies, she touched him on the arm.

"Jimmy—I think I'd better get on home. Mama will want me to help fix supper."

"All right," her brother said hurriedly. "But tell Mama not to set a plate for me. Mr. Wright has just given me a job helping around here. So I expect it'll be late when I get home."

"I'll milk Fanny for you tonight," Clara offered.

"Gee, thanks," Jimmy said, and raced off toward the supply tent.

Clara turned and walked slowly back across the dunes toward home.

The plain supper of bacon and beans was finished, and Jimmy was washing the tin plates from which the three had eaten. As he worked, he listened carefully to every word the Wrights were saying.

The brothers sat at the table under the light of a large oil lamp that hung from the ceiling. Wilbur was holding a small, ten-inch model of their glider in his hands, turning it over, inspecting it from every angle, as though trying to force the secret of flight from it by the sheer power of concentration.

"Orv," he said finally, "we might as well face up to the facts. You nor I nor anybody else is going to build a man-carrying glider, or a powered flying machine either, that will fly worth a nickel until we learn how to control it in the air. We'll never be able to control it till we lick the problem of balance."

He kept looking at the little model.

"I can't help feeling that the answer is right here, staring us in the face, if only we knew where to look for it."

Orville laughed.

"I'd say we've looked just about every place there is, Will."

"That's so. We've done a lot of looking. Maybe we just haven't been able to see what we were looking at."

Jimmy had finished the dishes and cleaned up the corner of the shack that served as a kitchen. Now he came over and sat on a wooden box, well back from the table but near enough so that he could hear all this fascinating talk.

"We've learned a lot, Orv, and that's for certain," Wilbur went on, talking as much to himself as to his brother. "We've learned that if a glider is well built and well designed, and if the wings are correctly curved to get maximum lift from the air-stream—we've learned that if all these things are done right, the glider will slide up or down a smooth, steady column of air. But let the wind change just a little bit, either in direction or velocity, and—whammo! That's the end of your glider."

"That's just what happened to my kite today."

Jimmy was so wrapped up in what Wilbur was saying that the words slipped out before he could stop them.

Orville turned around.

"Oh, it's you, Jimmy. I thought you'd cleaned up and gone home."

"N-no," Jimmy stammered, mentally kicking himself for not being able to keep his big mouth shut. "I—well, I was interested in what you were talking about."

"Well, if your pa and ma don't mind, you're welcome to stick around as long as you like. From the one quick look I had at that little glider of yours today, you know quite a lot about flying yourself."

Jimmy liked these young men from Ohio. They made him feel at home, made him feel important. And best of all, they had wonderful, crazy, exciting ideas. Now he felt emboldened to enter the conversation.

"When my kite—I mean my glider—smashed this afternoon, I was thinking the same thing that you were just talking about. As long as the wind was nice and steady, it flew like a bird. But when the wind changed, there was no way I could hold it."

"You just now put your finger on the whole problem, kid," Wilbur remarked drily, "when you said 'flew like a bird.' The birds know how to fly, but the question is, how do they do it? Doggone it, Orv! There must be *something* the birds do naturally that we could copy mechanically. They've got the secret. All we have to do is find it."

Orville chuckled and said to Jimmy:

"Will and I have spent I don't know how many hundreds of hours lying stretched out on our backs in the pasture near our house at home, watching the hawks and crows. But we still haven't found their secret."

"So have I," Jimmy replied. "I watch the gulls. They're the best fliers in the world."

"We've been watching them too," Orv said. "But, so far, your Carolina sea gulls haven't taught us any more than our Ohio crows."

"Jim," Wilbur said, "there's a case of soda pop out in the tent. As long as we're going to sit here gabbing, why don't you run out and get us each a bottle?"

"And while you're at it," Orville added, "you'll find a shoebox out there tied up with a string. It's got my new slippers in it. Bring them in with you when you come."

Jimmy lighted a lantern and went out to the supply tent. In a few minutes he returned carrying three bottles of pop and the shoebox. Wilbur opened the pop bottles and passed them around, while Orv took the slippers out of the box and put them on his feet.

"Ah-h! That's better!" Orv sighed as he laid the empty box on the table. "Running around on that hard sand in high-cut shoes makes a man's dogs start to bark."

"You're getting soft, Orv." Wilbur laughed. "You spend too much time lying on your back watching the birds. The sand doesn't bother Jimmy and me, does it, youngster?"

Jimmy didn't want to take sides, even in what he knew was friendly brother-to-brother joshing, so he laughed too, and said:

"Well, I was born here on this spit. I didn't know there was such a thing as soft, green grass till I was ten years old."

"Just the same," Wilbur repeated, "I think Orv spends too much time watching the birds."

Jimmy sipped his soda pop thoughtfully.

"You know," he said, during this lull in the talk, "getting back to birds, I've noticed one thing about gulls. When they want to change direction, they sort of lift up one wing. Now I wonder if you could figure out a way . . ." His voice trailed off, and he took another sip from the pop bottle.

"You mean," Wilbur suggested, "a way to make the wings move up and down, like on a hinge?"

"Yeah," Jimmy said, thinking about it. "Yeah. Maybe something like that might just do the trick."

"You're a smart boy, Jim." Wilbur grinned. "It took Orv and me a lot longer to think of that than it did you. But we tried it," he shook his head, "and it just doesn't work. It was Orv's idea, and he's still got it in the back of his head."

"If a bird flies by moving its wings," Orv insisted, "it looks to me like that's the logical way for a flying machine to do it."

"Nope," Wilbur said emphatically, "I think that's where all the flying machine people have been going wrong all these years. I'll admit that flapping its wings is what makes a bird get off the ground and stay in the air. But the engine will never be built that can move a pair of flying machine wings as fast as a bird can flap his. We've scrapped about this point a thousand times, Orv, and you know I'm right."

"With a capital W," Orv said, laughing, "you're Wright. But *without* the W, I'm not so sure you're right."

"Twenty-three skidoo for you, kiddo!" Wilbur said. "Go down to the store and buy yourself another joke. You've worn that one plumb out."

"Don't pay any attention to him, Jim," Orv said. "We do this all the time."

"That's right, without the W," Will agreed. "We get most of our good ideas this way."

"I wasn't thinking of flapping the wings to make the glider go," Jimmy said seriously. "I was only thinking of maybe tilting the wings a little bit to keep it balanced in the air."

"I know you were, Jim," Wilbur said. "We

gave up on wing motion for motive power a long time ago. Orv just likes to fun me about it. And we've tried the idea of tilting the wings on a hinge to keep the glider balanced. But all it does is throw the whole thing clean out of kilter. First we tried hinging the whole wing, and then we hinged a part of it. But every time, the glider acted just like we'd taken one wing clear off. No," he went on, shaking his head and draining the last of his soda pop, "hinging the wings just doesn't seem to be the answer. But I'll be hanged if I know why. It sure does seem reasonable when you talk about it."

Will put down his pop bottle and picked up the little model again, and began once more to turn it over and over in his hands. Without knowing that he was doing it, Jimmy picked up the top of the shoebox in the same manner.

"Now you take Otto Lilienthal," Wilbur continued. "He got himself killed because he tried to ride a glider before he'd ironed all the wrinkles out of it."

"Killed?" Jimmy gasped. "Did you say Lilienthal was killed?"

"That's right, Jim," Orv said. "Lilienthal made more free glides than anybody else, and set the record for staying up in the air for thirty seconds. But when he tried to break his own record, his glider stalled, just as yours did today, and crashed. Instead of breaking his record, Lilienthal broke his neck."

"My gosh!" Jimmy breathed, and suddenly the thought came back to him of what could have happened if he'd been riding on the lower wing of his kite today.

"Yep," Wilbur nodded gravely, "this flying business can be dangerous. You know what they say. Everything that goes up must come down. The trick is to keep it up till you want it to come down, and then to bring it down nice and easy."

"And also," Orville added, "the trick is to make your flying machine change directions in the air, either from side to side or up and down. I still think the only way to do it is with some kind of hinge, and some of these days we're going to find out how. You mark my words, Will." And then as an afterthought he added: "And you too, Jim."

As the brothers talked, Jimmy had been idly twisting the cardboard top of the shoebox in his hands, bending its ends from side to side in opposite directions. Suddenly, in the middle of a sentence Wilbur stopped talking. His long, lean jaw hung down, open-mouthed, and he began slowly to lean forward in his chair, staring fixedly at the boxtop as though hypnotized by it.

Jimmy inadvertently sat back and dropped his hands into his lap.

"No! No!" Wilbur almost shouted, his voice shrill with excitement. "Keep on doing that, boy! Go ahead! Keep on!"

Jimmy had no idea what he was talking about.

"K-keep on doing what?"

"Keep twisting that boxtop! Keep twisting it like you were."

"Was—was I twisting it? I don't know what you mean, Mr. Wright."

"Here!" Wilbur snatched the piece of cardboard from the boy's hands and held it for a long second before his staring eyes. Then, very slowly and deliberately, he began to twist it as Jimmy had been doing unconsciously a moment before. Still twisting and warping, he began to move the boxtop up and down and from side to side.

"What in the name of sense has come over you, Will?" Orv said. "Have you gone batty?"

"Orv," Will said, and now his voice had become low and tense. "Holy, jumpin' frogs, Orv! We've got it! So help me, I think we've got it! Look here!"

He took a penknife from his pocket and trimmed off the sides of the boxtop, leaving only a flat area of cardboard.

"Orv, you were right about your hinge all

along. But where we went wrong was that we were thinking of a hinge as if it were—well, as if it were a *hinge*. Now what *is* a hinge really? It's a twist."

He bent one corner of the cardboard down and the opposite corner up.

"Now let's say this is the wing of a glider, or a flying machine. When I warp this corner down, I'm getting the same effect as if it were hinged. But instead of making a clean break in the surface, the way a regular hinge would, I'm twisting it real easy. And I can give it a big twist or a little twist, just as much as I need and no more."

Still staring at the cardboard the way a charmed bird stares at a snake, he went on:

"With this corner twisted down, I twist the opposite corner up, and look what happens."

He moved the cardboard wing forward.

"The wind-stream catches this turned-down corner, and this turned-up one. That makes your wing kind of tilt, like this. And what happens? You change your direction."

Orville jumped to his feet and slammed his fist down on the table.

"Holy smoke, Will!" He brought a big hand down hard on his brother's shoulder. "That's it, boy! That's my hinge!"

Will nodded his head and grinned with satisfaction.

"Man, oh, man!" Orv shouted. "Now I see what the birds *really* do! They don't lift up their whole wing when they want to turn. They just twist up the feathers on the tip. And that makes them tilt, just like you said. Boy, have we been blind!"

"That's the truth, Mr. Wright!" Jimmie exclaimed. "That's the exact truth! Now that I think back, I've seen the birds do that a thousand times. Only I didn't know what I was looking at."

Wilbur laughed. "What's that verse from the Good Book that Pa quotes all the time, Orv? 'They have eyes, yet they see not.' That's been us."

Orville picked up the model that his brother had put down on the table when he reached for the cardboard.

"Look," he said, his voice high with excitement. "We can fasten wires to here, and—"

"Take it easy, Orv," Wilbur said. "Pa says it never hurts to sleep on a good idea for at least one night. It's getting late, so let's turn in and be fresh and clear-headed when we go to work on this in the morning."

CHAPTER THREE

The Wind Tunnel

THE early morning sun had only just begun to tint the eastern sky with brush strokes of pale pink when the crowing of a rooster in the chicken yard woke Jimmy with a start. He jumped out of bed and pulled on his clothes. The rest of the family was still asleep.

He tiptoed out of the house and set about his morning chores. First, he brought in a supply of cordwood for his mother's cookstove and piled it on the back porch outside the kitchen door. Then he took a measure of cracked corn down to the chicken house and collected the eggs. After that, he carried a pail out to the barn and milked old Fanny, the Blairs' family cow.

Now just one last chore remained. He went back to the barn and led Rock, his father's buggy-horse, out of his box stall. He cleaned the stall, then took a brush and currycomb from the tack-shelf and gave Rock his morning grooming.

As his hands moved swiftly over the horse's gleaming chestnut coat, Jimmy kept thinking about wings. Wings that could be warped or twisted so that a glider or a flying machine would go in any direction its driver wanted it to. All night, his fitful dreams had been filled with wings —soaring gulls and soaring gliders.

When he was all through, he put Rock back into the stall and forked down his breakfast of hay from the mow. He gave him a fresh bucket of water from the pump. Then Jimmy took his bicycle from its accustomed place just inside the barn.

The big red ball of the sun had edged up over the ocean now. Jimmy looked toward the house, but the family still seemed to be in bed. Well, he guessed Papa and Mama wouldn't be too angry if he failed to show up for Sunday School just this once. Besides, Clara would know where he was.

He jumped on his bike and pedaled furiously down the sandy road toward Kill Devil Hill.

When he entered the Wright brothers' shack, Orville was washing up the last of the breakfast dishes while Wilbur sat at the small table working on the little glider model with a penknife, scissors, tweezers, a reel of thin fish-line and a pot of bicycle cement. The first thing Jimmy did was make a grab for the dish towel in Orville's hand.

"Here, Mr. Wright," he said. "That's my job."

"I'm all done," Orville told him, smiling.

"That's right, Jim," Wilbur said. "Take it easy, and you'll live longer, Pa always says. Besides, boy, you earned more than your week's pay when you bent that boxtop last night. Unless I miss my guess, you put us on the right track at last."

"Pshaw!" Jimmy said, suddenly embarrassed. "I didn't even know what I was doing."

"That doesn't matter," Wilbur told him. "The important thing is that you did it. Now come over here and take a look at this."

Wilbur had carefully stripped the silk covering from the little model's wings, exposing the skeleton of thin ribs. He had then attached two lengths of fishline to each wing-tip and threaded them back through a tiny pulley.

"Now what I've done," he explained, "is work out a method of warping the wings so they will twist the way that box-top did last night. Now we fasten the threads to two small control handles like this—" his fingers were working dextrously as he talked—"and then we do like this." By twisting the handles and thus pulling the strings, he warped the little wing-tips first one way and then the other. "See?"

"Great gosh!" Jimmy gasped. "You mean you've rigged all that up just this morning?"

"There was nothing to it, Jim," Wilbur said good-naturedly, "once we'd found the basic principle. Besides, if you can fix a cranky bicycle, you can fix 'most anything."

"What do bicycles have to do with it?" Jimmy asked, puzzled.

Orv chuckled. "I guess we didn't have much time to get acquainted yesterday, Jim. Will and I run a bicycle repair shop back home in Dayton."

"Then you're not—not inventors?"

Now it was Wilbur's turn to laugh.

"We're bicycle fixers in the spring and summer, and flying machine makers during the fall and winter when it's too cold for much bicycling."

He made a final adjustment to the little model's wing controls. Then, with a needle and fine silk thread, he began sewing the covering back on the frame.

"Now," he said, "we'll be ready in a minute to try her in the wind machine."

Jimmy watched closely as Wilbur's skillful fingers re-sewed the silk over the ribs. When he was finished, he held the model up in one hand and looked it over from every angle.

"Well," he said finally, "she'll either work or she won't, and we'll soon find out which."

He got up and went over to a curious contraption on the workbench. It was a square wooden box, about two feet high, two feet wide and eight feet long, with glass windows built into its sides and top. Both ends were open, but a metal fan, driven by a small gasoline motor, was rigged up at one end to send air through the tunnel.

"What in the world is that?" Jimmie asked.

"That's our wind machine, or wind tunnel, as Orv calls it. We figured it out last year when we were fooling around with Orv's hinged-wing theory. You see, it doesn't make any sense to waste time building a full-sized glider until you know how the wing design is going to react to a stream of air."

As he talked, he reached into the back of the box and suspended the little glider model on wires. Then he threaded the control lines through slits in the side.

"I think that where people like Professor Langley, of the Smithsonian Institution, and Dr. Alexander Graham Bell, and all the others who've been working on flying machines have gone wrong is that they figure out a design on paper that they think should work. And then they build their full-scale machine. When it crashes, they go back over their arithmetic, decide what they did wrong, and then build another machine. Of course, they have a lot of money to fool with, so

they can afford to do it the hard way. But Orv and I have to watch every penny. We can't afford to build a big glider until we have some reason to believe that it will behave the way we want it to in the air. So we make a model first, and try it out in the wind tunnel. This gadget is far from perfect. But if it won't always tell us what is right, it shows us what is wrong every time."

Orville was tinkering with the gasoline engine, getting it primed to start the fan.

"We tried a lot of things before we thought of this wind tunnel," he put in. "First, we swung our models around on a string, but we saw right away that was no good."

Jimmy was taking elementary physics in high school, and now he nodded sagely, eager to contribute something, to let the Wrights know that he knew what they were talking about.

"Of course not," he said. "You'd have your string pulling the glider one way, and centrifugal force pulling it the other."

Wilbur looked up and shrugged his shoulders.

"You're just a kid, Jim," he said, "and you saw that right away. Neither Orv nor I ever got beyond high school, and we saw it too. But Langley, for all that he's a great scientist, can't see it—any more than, up to last night, we could see that the gulls were lifting up their wing-tips instead of their whole wings."

"That's right, Jim," Orville added. "Langley and Bell, too, have based all their principles of aerodynamics on experiments that are entirely different from ours, and we think we're way ahead."

"It was Orv," Wilbur went on as he adjusted the fish-line controls of the little model, "who thought of the wind tunnel. The only force exerted on a glider or a flying machine that means anything is the force exerted by the air in free flight. So Orv figured that if you can't move your model through the air, then why not move the air against your model? It sounded like it ought to make sense, and by golly, when we tried it, it worked."

He had finished his adjustments now. So, taking the lines that controlled the model in his fingers, he said: "All right, Orv. Turn her over."

Orville began to crank the engine. It coughed, spat, sputtered, wheezed, and finally caught. Orv adjusted the throttle until it was humming along at a slow, even rate. The fan began to turn, sending a flow of air through the wooden tunnel and against the leading edges of the glider's wings. Wilbur made sure once again that he was holding the control strings the way he wanted them. The little model shivered slightly, but held steady.

"Now give me just a hair more," Will ordered.

Orville advanced the throttle a notch, and the speed of the air-flow increased.

"All right, boys," Wilbur said, "keep your fingers crossed. Here we go."

Although the morning air in the shack was cool, Jimmy could see beads of perspiration standing on Wilbur's forehead.

Slowly, gently, very delicately, Wilbur worked the control strings with his fingers. The rear tip of the right wings warped slightly upward, and the tip of the left wings slightly downward. Smoothly, evenly, just like a soaring gull, the little glider model put its left wings up and banked toward the right, as far as the wires from which it was suspended would permit.

Not a word was spoken, and the two men and the boy watched in breathless silence as Wilbur reversed the controls. The model straightened up to an even keel, and then banked slowly to the left. Wilbur leveled it off again. The glider, as sensitive to the controls as a gull to the uplift of its wing-tips, soared on the moving column of air.

Will repeated these maneuvers over again several times, and then Orville could no longer stand the strain of the excitement that was bursting inside him.

He jumped up and whooped:

"Yow-ee! It works, Will! It works!"

Then he began doing an Indian war dance around the room, yipping and yelling as he jogged up and down. He gave Will a shove as he passed, and the older brother dropped the control strings and shoved him back, grinning from ear to ear.

"Come on, Will! Come on, Jim!" Orville shouted. "Holler and whoop it up! We've got a glider that flies!"

"Wait a minute, Orv!" Will said. "Hold your horses! We've got a little old ten-inch model that flies. That doesn't mean we've got a man-sized glider by a long shot. So don't count your flying machines before you see 'em in the air."

This thought sobered Orv a little and he said: "But, heck, Will! The model worked. That means the glider will work too."

"All it means, Orv," Will told him seriously, "is that the glider *ought* to work. But first, we've got to take it down and re-rig it."

His voice became very businesslike.

"Jimmy, while Orv and I are taking the cloth off the wings, you run into the store in town and get a reel of heavy piano wire and a bolt of this kind of muslin. I'll cut you a sample. We need this—"

"But this is Sunday, Mr. Wright," Jimmy reminded him. "The stores aren't open."

"Oh thunder!" Will said. "That's right."

"But I expect Mr. Porter, the piano tuner, has

some piano wire at his house. I'll run into town and see."

Will rubbed his hands together briskly.

"Good boy, Jim. You do that."

"But I'm afraid we'll have to wait till the store is open tomorrow to get the cloth."

"All right. Orv and I can get started on the framework." He snapped his fingers, suddenly remembering something. "We're going to have to have a sewing machine to stitch the wing covering. Do you have any idea where we could rent one for a day or so?"

Jimmy brightened.

"Why, sure," he said. "My mother has a new machine she'll be glad to lend you. And my sister Clara is just about the best seamstress in town."

"Jimmy," Wilbur grinned, "I told you it was good luck for us when you showed up at this camp. Now hightail it out of here and see if Mr. Porter has that piano wire."

Jimmy bolted from the shack, vaulted onto his bike, and wheeled off down the dry, sandy road in a cloud of dust.

CHAPTER FOUR

Clara Lends a Hand

IT was late afternoon of the following day, and the shack at the camp of the Wright brothers was bristling with furious activity. Clara sat at the sewing machine, surrounded by yards of the muslin wing-covering material. Her foot worked steadily on the treadle, and her slender fingers industriously fed the pieces of cloth, which Orv had cut out for her, into the clicking needle.

Orville and Wilbur worked on the bare framework of the wings—attaching the warping wires and threading them through a series of pulleys, repairing the rudder smashed in Saturday's spill.

Jimmy was their helper and general handyman —fetching tools, holding things straight, making himself useful however he could, and working as hard at it as either of the Wrights.

Clara sat surrounded by yards of muslin

Everybody went about the job silently and intently. The only sounds were the steady hum of Clara's machine, and an occasional grunted "Will, give me a hand with this strut," or "Jim, get us some more of those number-ten screws."

Just as the shadows were darkening inside the shack, with only a few precious minutes of daylight left, Clara got up from behind her machine and announced:

"It's all done, Mr. Wright."

Orville came over to inspect the job.

"I hope I did everything right," she said shyly.

Orv smiled, and patted her flaming red curls.

"It's right with a capital W," he said. "Tell your mama we'll bring the sewing machine back tomorrow."

"Mama says don't hurry. She says you can keep it as long as you need it."

"Then tell her thanks a lot. If what we've done today doesn't work, we'll have to do the whole thing over."

He took a silver dollar from his pocket.

"Here, go buy yourself something pretty."

While they were talking, Wilbur and Jimmy came up. Will picked up a section of the wing-covering and looked carefully at the seams.

"Good work! Good work!" He made a motion

as if to slap Clara on the back, man-style. Then, realizing what he was doing, he checked himself and patted her on the head as Orv had done.

"Yes, this is a good, sound job." He grinned. "It takes a woman's hand to stitch a seam, as they say. There's no mistake about that. Orv and I are all right with a wrench or a screwdriver. But when it comes to a needle, even a sewing-machine needle, our fingers are all thumbs."

Jimmy had seen how delicately Will's fingers had handled the needle when he sewed the covering on the little model, and he knew the tall man was only making this speech to please Clara. That's one reason why he liked the Wright brothers, he reflected. They were always so considerate of other people.

"Is there anything else I can do tonight?" he asked.

"No, I think we've done all we can," Wilbur replied. "Orv and I will finish with the frame in the morning and stretch this covering over the wings. We ought to be ready to try her out about the time you get here in the afternoon, Jim. The fellows down at the weather station told me that the wind would be steadiest around three."

"I'll be here, don't worry," Jimmy said, grinning.

As usual, Clara felt bashful and shy amid all this man-talk. But she forced herself to say:

"M-may I come too, Mr. Wright?"

"You certainly may," Wilbur assured her. "After all, part of this glider is yours. Now run along home, you kids, or your supper will be cold."

Jimmy took his bicycle from where it had been leaning against the wall of the shack.

"Hop up on the handlebars, Clara," he said.

Mr. Blair was sitting at the big kitchen table, reading a newspaper by the light of an oil lamp, when Jimmy and Clara entered the room. The sweet, spicy fragrance of chicken and dumplings arose from a large iron pot that Mrs. Blair was stirring on the stove.

Their mother looked up.

"Better go wash your hands and face, Clara. You're just in time to help me set the supper table. And you, too, Jimmy. My land! You've got dirt streaked all over yourself. I don't know how you manage to do it."

When the washing-up was done, Clara flew around the kitchen helping her mother, and Jimmy sat down at the table beside his father.

"I'm sorry I wasn't here to do the evening milking, Papa."

"That's all right, son. It isn't every day a boy gets an after-school job that pays three dollars a week. Clara and I don't mind milking at night. And that money will come in handy. We'll put it in the bank for you against the day you're ready for college. And it's good for a boy your age to learn to work."

"Well, I'll tell you, Papa," Jimmy confessed, "this job is really more fun than work. You ought to see the big gliding machine the Wrights have built. And Will and Orv have figured out a way to control it in the air."

Mr. Blair pushed his steel-rimmed specs up onto his forehead.

"I haven't had much of a chance to talk to you about these Wright fellows.
You've been out of

the house most of the time since you've met them. The thing I don't quite understand is why grown men come all the way down here from Ohio just to fly kites."

"They came to Kitty Hawk," Jimmy explained, "because the U. S. Weather Bureau told them this is where the steadiest winds blow. And they're doing a lot more than flying kites, Papa. They're building a real, man-carrying glider. Wilbur says that when they've got the glider so it will stay up in the air, like—" he groped for words to express what he was trying to say—"well, like a kite without a string, they're going to put an engine on it, so's it will stay up as long as they want it to, and go wherever they please."

Mr. Blair shook his head.

"It appears to me like lots of people are talking about flying machines, but up to now nobody is making them fly. I've just been reading in this week's paper about some professor up in Washington who's building one."

"That's Langley," Jimmy put in quickly, eager to show off his knowledge about flying machine matters in general. "But Orville says his machine can't possibly get off the ground. The aero—" he puckered his brows as he tried to remember the unfamiliar word—"the aerodynamics are all wrong."

"What are these aero-things?"

"Well," Jimmy admitted, "I'm not quite sure, Papa. But it has something to do with the way the air currents act on a pair of wings to keep a machine in the air. Orville says the aerodynamics of a sea gull are perfect."

His father laughed.

"Well, boy, when the Good Lord made sea gulls, he made them so they could fly. And I reckon if he had wanted humans to fly around in the air, he'd have put wings on them too."

"But that's what the Wrights are doing, Papa," Jimmy persisted loyally. "They're making wings that men can fly with. Wilbur says he reckons that man ought to be able to build a machine to do mechanically what the birds do naturally."

"You quote these Wrights a good deal, son," Mr. Blair said. "What kind of people are they anyway, that is, if they aren't just plumb crazy?"

"They're sure not crazy," Jimmy said emphatically. "They're the greatest guys I've ever met. They act like there isn't a thing in the world that can't be done if somebody is just smart enough—and tries hard enough to find a way to do it. And they're the best mechanics I ever saw. Why, you ought to see some of the things they've built."

He told his father about the wind tunnel, and how the little model had flown in it perfectly, turning up the tips of its wings to balance itself like a bird.

"Well, I'll be switched!" Mr. Blair exclaimed. "It took a real smart man to figure that one out, sure enough!"

"That's what I'm saying, Papa. Both the Wrights are *real* smart men. Just about as smart as they come."

As father and son had been talking, Clara bustled around setting the dishes and the silver on the table.

Then Mrs. Blair called out:

"All right, everybody! Supper's ready!"

For the next half hour, Jimmy's interest in flying machines took second place to his interest in chicken and dumplings.

Maybe a chicken's wings weren't made for flying, but, boy! they sure did taste good!

CHAPTER FIVE

The Glider

J IMMY was having a hard time concentrating on what the teacher was saying as he sat fidgeting behind his desk in physics class. His body was here in the high school classroom. There was no doubt about that. But his mind was four miles away by the windy slopes of Kill Devil Hill.

Suddenly, one of the teacher's questions yanked his mind back into the classroom.

"Now, class," the teacher was asking, "can anyone explain the difference between centrifugal and centripetal force?"

Jimmy's hand shot up.

"All right, Jimmy. You may tell us."

Jimmy arose from behind his desk, and stood up in the approved manner for reciting in class.

"Centrifugal force is the force that pulls *outward*. Centripetal force is the force that pulls *inward*."

"Very good. Now give us an example."

"Suppose," Jimmy said, "that I have an object, like—like, well a model glider—tied to the end of a string. Then I swing it around my head like this." He demonstrated. "Now, centrifugal force keeps trying to throw the glider off in a straight line, on a tangent to the circle. And centripetal force, which is exerted by the string, keeps pulling it back toward the center of the circle."

"Excellent, Jimmy. Are there any questions, class?"

"I have one myself," Jimmy said.

"Very well. Proceed."

"We know," Jimmy began rather uncertainly, "that when centrifugal force and centripetal force act against each other, it is possible to keep any object, even a piece of rock, going around in circles through the air. But is there any force that could keep an object like, say, a flying machine, going along through the air in a straight line?"

The teacher looked perplexed for a moment, and then he smiled.

"That's a curious question, Jimmy, but I'll try to answer it for you. The answer is a simple no.

I'm sure you have been reading all this nonsense in the newspapers about flying machines. I have too. But there's one force that these flying machine people forget about. And that's the force of gravity. A rifle bullet, or a baseball will fly along in what appears to be a straight line for a short distance. But when its forward motion is spent, it always falls back to earth. That's Newton's First Law, class. And that's why nobody will ever build a machine that can fly. So I wouldn't worry any more about such claptrap as flying machines, Jimmy. Instead, I suggest that you give some thought to tomorrow's lesson, which will be . . ."

As the teacher talked on, Jimmy's thoughts wandered out the open window of the classroom, and flew—in a straight line, never once falling to earth to accommodate Sir Isaac Newton—back to Kill Devil Hill.

Half an hour later, Jimmy was rapidly pedaling his bike down the sandy road, with Clara once again perched on the handlebars. He sure hoped they'd get to the camp before the Wrights tried out the new glider!

As he rounded the base of the hill, he saw the brothers carrying the glider out of the shack. The white muslin covering, stretched over the framework of the wings, gleamed in the afternoon sun.

"Hi, kids!" Orville called, waving his hand. "You're just in time."

Jimmy leaned the bike against the shack and ran to lend a hand. The three of them hauled the glider to the top of the hill and set it down carefully on the brim of the slope. Wilbur took two

strands of stout line that were attached to the lower right wing in his hands. Orville did the same on the other side of the glider.

"Now, Jim," Will said, "you stay here and hold

her steady, while Orv and I go down the hill and pay out our lines. When I say go, release her. Got that?"

"Yes, sir," Jimmy said, steadying the wings of the huge glider and holding it firmly on the sand.

The Wrights walked down the hill, keeping their lines tight—in much the same way, Jimmy thought, as he had done on Saturday when Clara was holding his kite for him. Then, when the wind was nice and steady, Wilbur yelled:

"Go!"

Jimmy released his hold, and as Orville and Wilbur pulled on their lines, the glider soared up into the air as prettily as any sea gull. It hovered for a moment, balanced delicately on the steady stream of air that flowed against the slope of the hill.

Then, working their controls in unison, the Wright brothers began putting their machine through its paces. First, it lifted up one wing and banked. Then it lifted the other and banked in the opposite direction. Answering instantly to the controls as Orv and Will manipulated them, the frail craft danced and cavorted on the updrafts like a leaf on the surface of a stream. Then the brothers straightened it out, and once more it rode the wind steady and straight and firm.

"Okay, Orv," Wilbur shouted. "Let's bring her down."

They pulled on the lines, and the glider came lightly to earth.

Jimmy, with Clara behind him, raced down the slope. Wilbur and Orville each wore a smile as wide as his face. But this time there was no whooping and yelling. This time there was only a quiet feeling of inward satisfaction—the satisfaction of knowing that, after all these trying years, they were at last coming close to the magic key that might unlock the secrets of flight.

They carried the glider back to the top of the hill.

"Now, Jim," Wilbur said, pointing to a pair of cement sacks, "fill those up with sand and tie them securely."

Jimmy didn't ask questions. Anything the Wrights wanted him to do, he did automatically. He began to scoop sand into the sacks, and Clara ran to help him.

The sacks, when they were full, weighed about seventy-five pounds each. Still wondering what this was all about, Jimmy helped Will and Orv lash them to the lower wing of the glider.

Then Wilbur explained:

"As you know, Jim, the object of all our experiments has been to develop a glider that will safely carry a man. Otherwise, all you've got is a kite that is of no practical use to anybody. We think we've got the problem of balance licked, thanks to the warping wings. Now we want to see how she'll behave when she's carrying a payload."

Once again, Jimmy held the glider steady until the Wrights pulled her off the brink of the hill. And again she flew perfectly, riding the wind with all the grace of a winged horse. She banked, leveled, and straightened out again—answering promptly to every command that Will and Orv sent up her controlling lines.

They pulled her down for the second time, and Wilbur looked at Orv and said:

"I want Jimmy to try it with my controls this time."

Jimmy gasped, but he said nothing. His heart leaped up at this tacit evidence that he was being accepted on an equal footing with Will and Orv, that he was one of the team.

"Now you helped install these controls, Jim," Wilbur said earnestly. "So you know how to work them. But let's go over the procedure once more. When Orville yells: *'Left!'* you pull this line here. That warps your wing-tip down while he warps his up. When he yells: *'Right!'* you pull *this* line. And that makes the glider do just the opposite. When he yells: '*Steady!*' you even the lines. Is that clear?"

Jimmy nodded. His breath was coming hard, and he had to wipe his palms on his pants to get rid of the sudden sweat that was making them slippery. Wilbur and Orville were trusting him with their precious glider! He couldn't fail them now, and, by golly, he wouldn't!

"Okay," he said, gathering the control lines in his hands. "Let her flicker!"

The glider went up easily, as it had before. It pulled against Jimmy's lines, the way a spirited horse fights for his head. And it responded to the pressure of his fingers on the controls just as a good horse responds to the hands of an expert rider.

After five minutes, during which the glider worked perfectly, Wilbur gave the signal, and Jim and Orville pulled the craft back down to earth.

Wilbur nodded his head happily, and grinned his big, white-toothed grin.

"I think we're ready, don't you, Orv?"

"We're as ready as we'll ever be, Will."

"Well, Jim," Wilbur said, "this is what we've been doing all our work for. I wanted you to get used to the controls because the next time, instead of a couple of sacks of sand, I'm going to ride her."

Wow! A pulse started to beat so hard in Jimmy's

throat that it actually ached. It was one thing to handle the controls when the glider was carrying a sand-weight. But with Will Wright riding it . . .

"Now don't get nervous, Jim," Will said comfortingly. "You did just fine, and it won't be any different with me on board. Just hold her nice and steady, and don't yank on your control lines. Pull 'em easy, just the way you did the last time."

At the top of the slope, Wilbur lay prone in the middle of the lower wing. His hands gripped the leading edge, and his feet were braced near the trailing edge.

Jimmy and Orv took their lines down the hill as before, and on Will's signal, pulled the glider into the air.

Everything was just as it had been when the sandbags, instead of a human passenger, were riding the wing. The glider responded to every command of the control lines, floating on the ocean of air as serenely as a bird.

After a few minutes, Wilbur yelled:

"All right! Lemme down!"

Jim and Orville pulled him back to solid ground.

When Will got up off the wing and regained his feet, Jimmy noticed that there was a trace of paleness under the deep tan of his face, but his smile was the contented, confident smile of a man who has finally achieved a lifelong ambition.

"Orv," he said softly, "that was the greatest thrill of my life. I wish Pa were here. I wish he could have seen it."

For a long moment, no further word was spoken. And then Orv said quietly:

"I guess I'd better try it."

Once more they pulled the glider up the hill, and this time it was Orville who stretched himself out on the lower wing.

His flight was as successful as Will's had been.

For the next hour, the brothers took turns making short flights on the glider. Each time, it behaved just as it was supposed to.

Finally, Jimmy could contain himself no longer.

"Mr. Wright," he said, his eyes begging, "may I have a crack at it?"

Wilbur grinned and shook his head.

"No, Jim. I'm sorry. Not you. This is a dangerous business, and I don't think your Pa would like it if we let you risk your neck."

Then, seeing the disappointment in the boy's face, and the tears that seemed just about ready to erupt, he clapped him on the shoulders and said: "Someday, Jim. Someday. But not now."

Once again he was all business. He looked up at the sky, and saw that the sun was still high. Then he held up the outstretched fingers of one hand to feel the wind.

"This seems to be our lucky day, Orv," he said. "And gambling men tell me that the time to press your luck is when it's running. Let's rig the controls so she can be handled from the air."

Orville nodded, then turned to Jimmy:

"Run down to the camp, Jim, and fetch the coil of light rope that you'll find in the tent."

When Jimmy got back to the top of the hill, Orville and Wilbur had connected the control lines to a saddle-like frame on the glider's lower wing, so that the rider could manipulate them by shifting his hips from side to side. Now Wilbur tied one end of the rope to the center of the front spar in the manner of a kite string.

Orville stretched out on the wing and worked the controls. They responded easily.

"Okay, Jim," Wilbur explained, "you and I are going to fly this thing like a kite. But Orv will be handling the controls himself. You all set, Orv?" Will turned to his brother.

"All set," Orville replied.

As before, Will and Jimmy took their line part way down the slope of the hill and pulled the glider

63

into the stream of air. The wings caught the up-flowing currents and rode them as a canoe rides the rapids in a river, with Orville up there at the controls, banking the glider, leveling it, swooping it up and dipping it down.

When they pulled him in at last, Orville's face was one big smile. "I think you've got something, Will," he said, "about this being our lucky day. So what say we go whole hog?"

Wilbur ran his hand thoughtfully over his nose and across his lean chin.

"Gosh, Orv! I don't know. We hadn't planned to move quite this fast."

"How much testing does she have to have, Will? She's behaving like a baby with a stick of peppermint candy. Come on, kiddo! Let's give 'er her head!"

"All right," Will said at last, giving in to Orv's persuasion without too much argument. "But I'll try her first."

"Oh, no, you won't," Orv said sternly. "I'm the only one who's handled her from the air. So if we aim to go it alone today, it's going to have to be me."

"I promised Pa that I'd take care of you," the older brother said.

"Yes," Orv grinned, "and I also promised him

that I'd take care of myself. So forget about it. Let's get going."

For about the dozenth time that afternoon, they pulled the glider back up the slope to the brink of Kill Devil Hill. But this time, when they straightened her out to face into the wind, she was as free as a bird about to take wing.

No lines, no ropes, nothing at all connected her with the ground. At long last, after years of toil and sweat and study and hard work, the Wright brothers, of Dayton, Ohio, were about to launch a free glider.

Orville stepped forward and stretched himself out on the lower wing. He grasped the control lever firmly in his hands and settled his hips in the saddle frame.

Then he turned around and grinned nervously at his brother.

"I just happened to think of something, Will. They call this place Kill Devil Hill. Devil kind of rhymes with Orville. I hope from now on they don't start calling it Kill Orville Hill."

Wilbur laughed.

"Twenty-three skidoo for you, kiddo!"

But Jimmy noticed that there was a tenseness in his face as he spoke, and a grim set to his lips.

"Now here's the ticket, Jim," Wilbur said

briskly. "When the wind is just right, I'll give the signal. You and I will each have hold of a wing-tip. At my word, we'll run down the hill and launch her into the air. I'll say 'Now!' when I want us to start running with her, and 'Go!' when I want you to let go. Have you got that?"

Jimmy nodded yes.

"Now it's very important that we both let go at the same time," Wilbur went on. "Otherwise we might slew her around right at the beginning."

"Yes, sir," Jimmy said, his heart pounding so hard that he could hardly speak.

"All right," Wilbur asked. "Are you ready, Orv?"

"I couldn't be readier, Will."

"Then good luck, kid!"

Jimmy held on firmly to the tip of the lower left wing. Will did the same on the right. Jimmy kept looking, first at Will, and then down the slope at the smooth, hard-packed sand over which he would have to run. The wind slackened for a moment, and then freshened in a steady gust.

Will waited one second, two, three, until he was sure that the breeze was going to hold steady.

Then he sang out: "Now!"

And he and Jimmy ran down the hill, carrying the glider between them.

Almost instantly, the little craft was sliding through the air, completely weightless. It was like holding a piece of paper. Jimmy tried to keep one eye on the slope ahead of him and the other eye on Will.

Then he heard Will's voice: "Go!"

He let go of his wing-tip and leaped clear.

The glider soared up to a height of about thirty feet, riding the river of air that flowed in from the sea. For a moment it held steady and sure. Then a changing gust of wind hit it, and it began to wobble. Orv put up a wing and straightened it out. Again it began to wobble, and again Orv compensated by putting up a wing. But this time the wind caught the rigid tail rudder and swept it around and then down.

The glider swooped up into the wind and came to an almost dead stop. Then, like a boy sliding down a banister, it slid backwards down the airstream and slammed tail first into the ground. The rear rudder crumpled, and the muslin-covered wings folded up like an accordion, hiding Orville's prone body from view.

Clara, watching from the top of the slope, screamed. Jimmy heard a voice yell. He wasn't sure whether it had been his or Will's. Then both of them were running toward the smashed glider.

As they got to it, Orville emerged into view, crawling backward from the wreckage. He stood up, teetering a little on his feet, shaking his head hard and rubbing his left shoulder.

Will took his arm. "Are you all right, boy?"

Orv shook his head again, as though to clear away the cobwebs that the crash had spun across his brain.

"That sand is mighty hard, Will."

Jimmy looked sadly at the ruins of the glider. Seconds before, it had been a graceful, living, vibrant thing. Now it was a tangled mass of wire and wood and cloth. What had happened? On the last flight, when he and Will had been holding it with the rope, it had flown as straight and true as an eagle. But once in free flight, entirely independent of the ground . . .

Then a thought hit him, and he said out loud:

"Centripetal force!"

"What's that, Jim?"

Orville had shaken off the temporary shock of his fall, and now he and Wilbur were gloomily inspecting the shattered remains of their glider.

"Centripetal force," Jimmy repeated, remembering the discussion in physics class that morning. "That's the force that pulls inward—that pulls things to the center of a circle."

"I don't get you, Jim," Orv said.

"I'm not sure that I get myself," Jimmy went on, trying to straighten out the jumbled thoughts that were crowding his head. "But when Will and I—" he wasn't aware that this was the first time he had used the familiar first name when speaking to either of the Wrights—"when Will and I were holding the rope, she flew fine. But we were exerting a force on her, a force that held her to the earth."

He scratched his head. "Gee, I don't know, Mr. Wright. I don't even know *what* I was thinking about."

"Well, whatever it was, Jim," Wilbur told him, "let's gather up this—this pile of trash—and lug it back to camp."

CHAPTER SIX

Free Flight

As a general rule, Jimmy Blair fell asleep the instant his head hit the pillow. But tonight he lay on his bed in his little room above the Blair kitchen and turned and twisted as the crash of the glider kept occurring over and over on the screen of his mind's eye.

What could have gone wrong? The warp-wing principle seemed to have solved all the Wrights' problems. The glider was behaving perfectly, answering to the controls like a well-trained show-horse. Then without warning, and for no apparent reason at all, the vagrant wind had caught the tail and slewed the glider around and smashed it into the ground. There must be an answer if only he could put his finger on it. He was trying futilely to unravel the riddle when sleep finally caught up with him.

But Orville Wright, lying on his cot in the shack

under Kill Devil Hill, was still awake. He couldn't sleep. He stared up into the darkness, mentally reliving every second of the disastrous flight.

The warped wings had worked like a charm. He'd had only to pull on the controls, and the glider straightened up instantly. The tail rudder was supposed to stabilize it, and keep it from side-slipping and skidding out of control. But, on the other hand, the wind had caught the stiff tail, and—

Suddenly he sat bolt upright, and the whole thing became crystal clear!

The tail rudder! There was the culprit! It was *rigid!* Making the tips movable had solved the wing problem. So make the rudder movable too! Hinge it! Rig it up with the same controls that warped the wings! Then it would work *with* the wings and not *against* them! This is what the gulls did when they spread their tail feathers. Here was the mysterious force that young Jimmy had tried to put a name to, the force that stabilized the glider when they flew her on a rope!

He jumped out of bed and yelled:

"Will! I've got it!"

His brother sat up and rubbed the sleep out of his eyes as Orville talked excitedly, the words spilling out almost faster than he could speak them.

"Don't you see, Will? Sailors have used movable rudders ever since boats were invented. The rudder exerts pressure on the water and keeps the boat on its true course. Air is like water, only not as dense. So turning the rudder with the wings will exert pressure on the air and keep the glider in balance!"

It was so simple that it sounded ridiculous.

Orv climbed into his clothes, fumbling for them in the dark, and then lighted the oil lamp.

"Holy cow, Will! Where have we been keeping our brains?"

Wilbur had caught the contagion of his brother's enthusiasm, and now he too got out of bed and began to put on his clothes.

"You know what Pa always says, Orv. Every problem is simple, once you have found the answer."

The remains of the wrecked glider lay in a corner of the shack. By the flickering lamplight, the Wright brothers began to sort out the pieces.

It was Saturday again, and once more the Wright glider sat poised on the brink of Kill Devil Hill. As before, Orville lay prone on the lower wing, his hand on the controls, and Will and Jimmy each had hold of a wing-tip.

Will and Orv, with Jimmy helping them every afternoon, had worked furiously for three days rebuilding the shattered frame. They hinged the rudder, and now it turned whenever the wings were warped. Clara had spent one long afternoon sewing a new muslin wing-covering. And now everything was ready for the final test.

"Ready, Orv?" Will asked.

Orville took a firmer grip on the controls and nodded his head.

"If she won't fly now," he said solemnly, "she's never going to, and we might as well give up and go back to fixing bicycles."

"That's right, kid, with a capital W," Will replied. "But something tells me that this time she's going to make it."

"I've got my fingers crossed," Orv said.

"So have I," Jimmy Blair added.

Then, at Orville's signal, he and Will launched the glider into the wind.

The little craft caught a current of air and sailed upward like a bird. A gust of wind hit it from the side and heeled it over, the way a sailboat leans into a breeze. Orv warped the wings, and at the same time the rudder came around to help them. The glider banked, came level again and floated on.

Wilbur yelled, and Jimmy found himself yelling too. The glider sailed on and on, with Will and Jim running along underneath it. Then Orv brought it down, and its runners touched lightly on the sand and skidded to a stop.

Orville got up from the wing, a big, satisfied smile spreading across his face.

"We've done it, boy! We've done it!"

Suddenly, Orv clapped his hand to his forehead.

"Oh, my gosh, Will!" he groaned. "Do you know what we've done? I'll bet we've broken Lilienthal's record, and we forgot to time ourselves. I'm sure I was up there more than thirty seconds."

"You were up there closer to a minute," Will said happily. "Let's try it again, and this time I'll hold a watch on you."

"No, I'll hold the watch," Orv said. "It's your turn. Go up there and break the record, kiddo."

Wilbur did. On his first glide, he sailed more than six hundred feet and stayed in the air forty-five seconds. Then Orville tried it again, and all the rest of the afternoon the brothers took turns with their new toy. They took the glider up, down and around in wide curves.

Finally Jimmy could contain himself no longer.

"Mr. Wright," he said to Wilbur, "isn't it about my turn?"

Wilbur shook his head, and the grin that had been on his face all day faded into a sober look.

"I'm sorry, Jim," he said. "You've earned it, and that's a fact. But as I told you, this is dangerous business. I can't take a chance. If anything happened to you, your pa would never forgive us. Someday, maybe. But not today. Now let's take this bird back to its nest."

Jimmy Blair sat across the table from his father, an intense fire burning in his eyes.

"Look, Papa," he begged, "you've just *got* to let me do it! If you give your permission, the Wrights will let me fly. And, Papa, I just purely have to take a ride on that glider before they go back to Ohio."

Mr. Blair pushed his glasses up onto his forehead.

"You really want to do this, don't you, son?"

"Papa," Jim said earnestly, "I want to do this

more than I've ever wanted to do anything in my life. Now that Orville fixed the tail, it's as safe as sitting in a rocking chair."

Mr. Blair drummed his fingertips on the top of the table.

"I don't think tom-fool gadgets such as flying machines or man-carrying kites will ever be safe. But then I don't think there's any sure way to keep crazy-headed boys safe either."

He grinned and scratched his chin.

"I remember once, when I was about your age, old Colonel Madison Mines, over in Elizabeth City, had a stallion colt that nobody could ride.

He offered ten dollars to the first fellow who could stay on him. I wanted to try it, but the old gentleman said I'd have to get my pa's permission before he'd let me risk my neck."

Jimmy had never heard this story before, but he knew that, right then, he was as good as lying on that glider wing.

"Did you stay on him, Papa?"

"I sure as thunder did," his father said. "But he was a lot of horse."

"This machine of the Wrights is a lot of glider, Papa. Look—you've never seen it. Why don't you come out with me in the morning and watch me take her up?"

"I just might do that, son," Mr. Blair said. "I reckon a man's never too old to learn a new trick."

"Now you listen carefully, Jim," Wilbur Wright said. "You know how to work these controls. But the thing is, you have to work them nice and easy. You don't jerk on the reins when you're riding a soft-mouthed horse, or on the handlebars when you're balancing a bike. So don't jerk on these controls when you feel her starting to dip. Just ease 'em, Jim. Feel her out."

"Yes, sir," Jimmy said.

His father and Clara stood on the top of the high dune, and now he glanced at them over his shoulder. His mouth was as dry and shriveled up as if he had taken a bite out of a green persimmon, and he desperately wanted a drink of water. He wondered if he'd lose his nerve once the glider got into the air. He sort of wished he hadn't talked himself into this, but it was too late to back out now.

Wilbur was at one wing-tip and Orville at the other.

"Ready, Jim?"

He grinned and nodded his head.

"All right, hang on." Orville grinned back. "Here you go."

The glider rode the column of air up to about forty feet. Down below him, miles down it seemed, Wilbur and Orville were running across the sand.

The glider dipped a wing with a sickening lurch. Jimmy eased the controls, and she straightened out on her course.

The wind sang in his ears and blew hard against his face. The muslin covering of the thin wings flapped and vibrated, and the airstream whistled around the struts.

It seemed as though time was standing still, as

His father and Clara stood on top of the high dune

if he had been in the air for hours, as if he had always been here. This was where he belonged! Up here in the limitless space of the blue sky. Not down on the ground, where something called gravity glued his feet to the earth; but up here with the gulls and the clouds, up here in another world. He felt full of confidence now, and all his fear left him.

He tried an easy turn, and the glider came around as obediently as old Rock when he was hitched to the buggy.

Then all of a sudden it dipped down toward the sand. For a split second, Jimmy was close to panic. But, almost instinctively, he brought the front rudder up. The glider leveled off, and then the runners were skimming across the sand, and digging up twin furrows.

Orv and Will ran up to him and helped him to his feet.

"Jim!" Orville was shouting. "You did fine, boy! Just fine! Will or I couldn't have handled her any better!"

"That was great, son! Just great! It sure beats riding a stallion colt!" his father exclaimed.

Clara didn't say anything. But her eyes were shining, and her fire-red hair was whipping in the wild wind.

Yes, Jimmy thought, it sure did beat riding any earthbound stallion! This was like riding Pegasus, the horse that flew through the air. He wanted to say something, but the right words wouldn't come. So he just stood there, with a foolish-looking grin on his face.

Wilbur broke the silence.

"Orv," he said, "I think we're about ready to put an engine on her this winter."

"Yep," Orv said, "I think we are."

CHAPTER SEVEN

The Flying Machine

1903

A BOY wearing the blue uniform of a Western Union messenger rode his bicycle into the Blairs' front yard. Clara, helping her mother with the dinner dishes, saw him first.

"Look, Mama," she said, pointing out the window. "Someone is sending us a telegraph message."

Mrs. Blair's hand flew to her throat.

"Oh, my stars!" she gasped. "I wonder what's happened. Maybe it's your Aunt Sally, down in Wilmington. She wrote last month to say she was feeling poorly."

By this time the messenger had stepped up on the porch and twisted the doorbell. The thin, tinny sound resounded through the house.

Mrs. Blair's face had become deathly pale.

"I declare, Clara! I'm afraid to go to the door."

"Maybe it isn't bad news at all," the girl suggested. Getting a telegram in the Blair household was indeed an unusual event. But she was eager to see who had sent it and what it was about.

"No," her mother persisted. "Nobody ever

sends a telegraph message unless it's bad news. I just hope it isn't your Aunt Sally, poor thing!"

Not ever having had reason to share her mother's dread of telegraph messages, Clara went to the door. The messenger boy tipped his cap, handed her a yellow envelope, then got back on his bike and pedaled down the road.

Clara looked at the envelope. It was addressed to Mr. James Blair, Jr., Nag's Head, Dare County, North Carolina.

"Mama," she cried. "It's for Jimmy!"

"Gracious!" Mrs. Blair exclaimed. "He's up in his room studying his lessons. Run and get him."

At that moment Jimmy himself came down the stairs. Clara handed him the envelope, and he tore it open. The telegram read:

DAYTON, O. SEPT. 17, 1903

ORV AND I ARRIVING KITTY HAWK SEPT. 25.

CAN YOU GET OLD CAMPSITE READY? HAVE

SURPRISE PACKAGE.

WILBUR WRIGHT.

Jimmy handed the wire to his mother, who had been hovering anxiously at his side.

"The Wrights are coming back," he announced, grinning happily. "I'd best get out to the camp first thing in the morning and see about putting it in shape. Between the mice and the wild razorback hogs, it's probably torn clean down to the ground."

"What do you suppose he means by a surprise package?" Clara asked.

"I dunno. Maybe a new glider of some kind.

Anyway, I'll have my hands full getting the camp ready for them."

"Do you want me to come with you?"

Jimmy pictured the shambles that the camp must have become during the past eleven months. He could use an extra pair of hands, there was no question about that.

"Why, sure," he said. "And I wouldn't wonder if they'll be needing you on the sewing machine again this year."

The shack beyond Kill Devil Hill was not quite as bad as Jimmy had expected. It was still standing, but the razorbacks had made a wreck of the inside. The workbenches sagged, the stove had been knocked over, and the legs of the table were broken. Grimly, Clara began to sweep out the year's accumulation of wind-blown sand and dirt, and Jimmy started repairing the damage.

The glider in which Will and Orv had made their experimental flights last fall had been lashed to the rafters of the roof, high up out of harm's way. And although the muslin-covered wings looked dusty and dirty, Jimmy didn't dare to try to take the glider down and clean it.

They had brought sandwiches for lunch, and so they worked straight through the day. By early evening, the camp was fairly presentable again.

"Tomorrow," Clara declared as they were getting ready to leave, "we'll bring out some soap and give it a good scrubbing down."

Jimmy met Orv and Will at the Kitty Hawk dock in the afternoon of the following Friday, and drove them and their huge pile of equipment and gear out to Kill Devil Hill in his father's buckboard behind old Rock. Thanks to Clara, the place was even more orderly than it had been eleven months before.

"Jim," Orville said as they bounced along the rutted road, "I hardly knew you. You must have sprouted up a foot."

Jimmy grinned self-consciously. It was true that he had grown taller in the year since the Wrights had seen him. Not a foot, but at least two or three inches.

"And how is that pretty little redheaded sister of yours?" Wilbur asked.

Jimmy explained how Clara had helped him get the shack in readiness.

"We're going to have another sewing job for her," Wilbur said.

"Another glider?" Jimmy asked.

"No, Jim," Wilbur said seriously. "This time we've got a real, honest-to-goodness, engine-powered flying machine. That's the surprise package we mentioned in our message."

Jimmy's eyes popped.

"Have you tried her out yet?"

"Not yet," Wilbur told him. "But we worked on the engine and the propellers all summer. And in the workshop, at least, they run perfectly."

"How does the engine make the glider go?" Jimmy asked eagerly.

"Wait till we get to camp," Orville put in. "Showing you will be easier than telling you."

At the shack, they unloaded the boxes and crates from the buckboard and carried them inside.

Wilbur looked at his watch.

"It's early yet," he declared. "So we might as well begin unpacking this stuff."

As they worked, Wilbur brought Jimmy up to date about the new flying machine they had built.

"Basically," he said, "the flying machine is very much like the glider we flew last year. But it's about five times as heavy."

Jimmy whistled.

"Gee! Isn't that too heavy to get off the ground?"

Wilbur shook his head.

"No, it's going to be carrying a twelve-horse-power engine and two big propellers. That will set up a mighty lot of vibration, so the frame has to be good and sturdy. We figure that if the aerodynamics of the machine are correct, the weight will be secondary."

"That's so," Orville chimed in. "If the machine's wings have enough lifting surface, and the engine has enough power, there's no reason why the whole thing couldn't weigh as much as a thousand pounds—or even a ton."

As he listened to the Wrights talk on about this amazing new flying machine of theirs, Jimmy felt as though he was right back in the same magical world of which he had been a part during the brief time he had worked with Will and Orv last year. He hadn't realized how much he'd missed all the wonderful and confident talk about their outlandish dream of conquering the air. It was almost, he thought, like when you went away on a long trip, and then came home again.

"So what we've done," Wilbur was saying, "is strengthen every part of the frame 'way beyond what we figured the margin of safety would be. We sure don't want the flying machine to fail because of a structural weakness. On the other hand, if we find we've made her too heavy for the engine's lifting power, we can always lighten her."

"We built the whole shebang in our workshop

at home," Orville explained, "right down to the last nut and bolt. Then we disassembled her for shipment down here. All we have to do now is put her back together."

Both brothers had been working as they talked, uncrating and sorting out a bewildering array of prefabricated flying machine parts—ribs, beams, struts, hinges, wires, rudders, cross braces, and rolls of muslin that would cover the wings.

Jimmy was hesitant about handling the actual parts of the machine, lest he do something that might damage them or throw their delicate adjustments out of kilter. So he took on the job of setting up the supply tent and carrying out the stores of tinned food that the Wrights had brought along.

By the time everything had been put in its proper place, the evening shadows inside the shack were lengthening, and Wilbur announced that it was about time to knock off for the day.

"You and I had better start thinking about supper, Orv," he said, "and you, Jim, ought to get that horse and wagon back to your pa."

"Mama told me," Jimmy said, "to invite you all to our house for supper, and to say that you're welcome to spend the night in our spare room."

Will shook his head.

"Tell your ma thanks very kindly, Jim. But I

don't think we ought to leave all this stuff out here overnight."

"Of course, Will," Orville said, winking at Jimmy, "I don't know that a nice, hot home-cooked meal ever hurt anybody. And besides, I haven't eaten anything on the train for the last four days but cold sandwiches."

Will grinned.

"Well, I suppose we could leave the place long enough to accept Mrs. Blair's hospitality.

"That's so," Orville agreed. "It wouldn't be polite to refuse. Then we can come back here for the night."

The elaborate meal of sizzling fried chicken, steaming yams, fragrant gravy, sweet cornpone, and a succulent assortment of every pickle and preserve that Mrs. Blair had in the root cellar—and all topped off with thick slabs of hot mince pie—was over at last. Jimmy, his father, and the Wright brothers sat in the living room while Clara and her mother cleaned up the few scraps that remained after the hungry men had declared that they'd had enough. As Orville had suggested earlier, four days of cold sandwiches on the train had honed the inventors' appetites to a razor edge.

Neither of the Wrights smoked, but Mr. Blair

asserted that no meal was complete without a pipe ful of tobacco as dessert. And so now thin clouds of blue smoke curled upward from his battered old corncob.

"As the boy here may have mentioned," he said, "I run a fishing supply store down by the wharf, and one day for me is pretty much like every other one. So I've never had time for any such shennanigans as flying machines. But I saw Jim ride your kite last fall, and he hasn't talked about much of anything else all year."

Wilbur's narrow face was serious as he tried to explain why two grown men, proprietors of a respectable bicycle business in a prosperous Ohio town, would devote so much of their time and hard-earned money to these crazy shenanigans.

"Well, sir," he began, "we first got interested in flying as a sort of a hobby. I guess it all started about four or five years ago when Orv had to spend a couple of months in bed after a siege of typhoid fever. He got to reading some books about the experiments that men like Chanute and Langley and Bell had been trying, and I suppose we just naturally caught the flying fever as a substitute, you might say, for Orv's typhoid fever."

"We'd always been interested in building kites," Orville added, "and so we just accidentally stumbled onto what we think is the answer to pow-ered flight. First build a man-carrying kite, or glider, that can be controlled in free flight. And then put an engine on it that will keep it in the air."

"I think I had better explain," Wilbur said, "that up to now, most flying machine people have been going at it in just the opposite way. They've been trying to build a steam engine, or a gasoline engine, powerful enough to pull anything, even a flat piece of metal, straight up into the air. And that just simply can't be done."

Mr. Blair tapped his pipe stem against his front teeth.

"I'm afraid you're way over this old storekeeper's head."

"Well," Wilbur said, "maybe I can make it simpler." He thought for a minute about how to simplify the theory of flight for someone who had never even thought about it before.

"Have you ever seen these little flying toys—something like a round lollipop stick with a little wooden fan-blade on top shaped like a ship's propeller?"

Mr. Blair nodded.

"You buy them in the candy store for a penny," Jim said.

"That's right, Jim. You hold the stick between the palms of your two hands, like this, and then as you spin it hard, you let go. The toy shoots up into the air maybe fifteen or twenty feet, and then falls back in a second or two after it's lost its speed."

Mr. Blair puffed on his pipe, and once more nodded.

"Now it's that kind of toy," Will continued, "that has been fooling most of the people who try to build flying machines. Can you imagine the size of the propeller, and the weight of the engine, and the amount of fuel it would take to keep a contraption like that up in the air—especially if it was big enough to carry a man?"

Mr. Blair shook his head sagely, still not quite clear in his mind as to what Wilbur was talking about.

Jimmy listened and drank in every word. He knew perfectly well what Wilbur meant.

"Now on the other hand," Will went on, "a kite will stay up as long as there's an upward breeze, and as long as it's controlled from the ground. A sea gull will stay up, even when there isn't a breeze, and control its own movements in the air. So Orv and I have tackled this business of flying from the standpoint of the kite and the gull, instead of the big locomotive-size engine. And you saw yourself how Jimmy, last fall, was able to keep our glider in the air for nearly a minute, and under perfect control all the time."

Mr. Blair began to pay closer attention. This was starting to make sense.

"When we left here a year ago," Wilbur said, "we figured we had most of the kinks and wrinkles ironed out of our glider. So what we've done now is build a glider big enough to carry an engine and two propellers that will push it through the air.

Not straight up; that's ridiculous. But *forward* through the air."

"You figure she'll work?" Mr. Blair asked.

"If everything goes the way we think it will, we're pretty confident that it's got a good chance."

Will got to his feet.

"But we've got a powerful lot of work to do before we're ready to try her," he said, "and it's getting late. So we'd better say thanks for the best supper we ever ate, and be getting along."

"I'll go hitch up Rock and drive you back to camp," Jimmy volunteered.

Orville laughed and shook his head.

"I think that after all that food the walk will do us good. But thanks anyway. Will we see you in the morning?"

Jimmy turned to his father.

"May I skip Sunday School tomorrow, Papa?"

Mr. Blair smiled at the eager, longing look on his son's face.

"I don't reckon you'd know what the teacher was saying anyway, your head would be so full of flying machines."

Jimmy brightened.

"I'll be there," he said to Orville, "before you're out of bed."

CHAPTER EIGHT

Trouble Hits Hard

WILBUR was right. There was a powerful lot of work to be done before the new flying machine would be ready to try its wings.

First, the engine had to be bench-tested to make sure it performed as well here in North Carolina as it had in the Dayton workshop. And by the time Jimmy Blair arrived at the Kill Devil Hill camp shortly after dawn the next morning, the brothers were not only out of bed, but were busy putting the engine together for a test run.

The block was made of aluminum, a bright, shining metal, not in general use, which Jimmy had heard about but never seen. Orv explained that it was lighter than steel, and, for its weight, even stronger.

"We had the dickens of a time getting an engine," he went on, talking as he worked. "First we tried to buy a light automobile engine, but there just wasn't any such thing. Weight isn't as important to a horseless carriage as it is to a flying machine."

Will laughed. "And when we tried to have one built to our specifications, people just thought we were plain looney. So we finally decided that if we wanted an engine we were going to have to build it ourselves. And that's what we did. Here, hand me that monkeywrench, Jim."

The job of putting the engine together—fitting the pistons, the valves, the magneto, and all the other mysterious pipes and arms and wires and moving gadgets that were complete Greek to Jimmy—went on through the lunch hour and well into the afternoon. Jimmy fixed sandwiches and coffee—Postum for Wilbur, who said that coffee made him nervous—and the Wrights wolfed the food down standing at the bench.

Again, it was late in the day before they were ready for the test.

Will primed the cylinders with gasoline, and then Orville attached a crank to the driveshaft and turned it over. There was a loud coughing and spitting and belching of blue-black smoke, and then the big twelve-horsepower engine caught with a bang and an explosive roar.

It was the worst racket Jimmy had ever heard, more noisy and raucous than the firing of a dozen rifles with a freight train passing by at the same time. The valves on the ends of the four cylinders jumped in and out too fast for Jimmy's eye to fol-

low them, and the two sprocket wheels on the driveshaft whizzed around at such furious speed that they became two spinning blurs.

In a few minutes, the shack was filled with a

cloud of oily, foul-smelling smoke. Just as Jimmy decided that he was going to have to run outside to keep from being sick, Wilbur flipped a switch and the engine grunted to a stop.

Orville noticed the peaked look on Jimmy's face.

"I think we'd all better get out into the open until this place airs out."

Once out in the fresh, salt-scented breeze that blew in from the sea, he went on:

"That engine wasn't designed to be run too long indoors, Jim. You see, we lubricate it with castor oil. Even the best petroleum oil is a little too heavy." He grinned. "And I don't have to tell you how sick an overdose of castor oil fumes could make you."

"I think a ride on your bike might clear the smell out of your nose, Jim," Wilbur said. "We need some fresh milk, so why don't you ride home and see if your ma can loan us a quart or two."

When Jimmy got back to camp with the milk, Orv and Will had already begun rigging up the frame that would support the two big propellers.

"We figure we'd better test everything right here on the bench," Orville explained when he saw Jimmy looking curiously at the framework they were building. "There's no sense in putting the flying machine together until we know for sure that the engine-and-propeller arrangement is going to work."

Will and Orv stuck to the job until it was too dark to see. Jimmy swept out the shack, carried in fresh water from the pump and fired up the cookstove. But from time to time he couldn't resist the urge to stop what he was doing and watch the Wrights.

Boy! he thought. It sure was hard to work in the same place where two men were building a flying machine!

"Well," Orv said as he washed the grime and grease off his hands when darkness finally forced them to quit, "we ought to have her ready for a run by this time tomorrow."

But it was nearly a week before the twin propellers were ready to turn.

First, a metal supporting brace snapped, and a day was wasted while Orv took it to a blacksmith in Nag's Head to have a replacement made.

Then the engine, which had worked so well the first time they tried it, began to get balky and contrary. Two of the four cylinders started to leak oil, and so the entire engine had to be laboriously dismantled and cleaned, the valves and pistons refitted, and then the whole thing put together.

Finally, as a last straw on the load of bad luck that had been dogging them all week, Wilbur accidentally banged one of the propeller blades with a heavy wrench and put a dent in its shining surface. And there went another frustrating day of pains-taking carving, planing, and sanding until the blade was once more perfectly smooth.

The propellers were far more fascinating to Jimmy than the engine itself. They would provide the driving force to pull the flying machine into the air and keep it there. Without them, the flying machine was nothing more than a giant-size glider, completely subject to the whims of the fickle winds.

Each propeller was made of three strips of two-by-four spruce wood glued together. Then the triple thickness of wood had been carefully cut and shaped by hand to the exact design that had proved most efficient in the Wrights' wind tunnel tests with models. The blades were more than eight feet long, and so thin that they looked ridiculously frail for the job they had to do.

Both Orville and Wilbur enjoyed talking to Jimmy. He wanted so desperately to learn everything there was to know about flying machines that he was the perfect listener. And now and then, as had been the case when he twisted the shoebox lid last fall, he asked questions out of sheer curiosity that in turn sparked ideas in the inventors' heads.

Now, as Wilbur sat patiently working on the damaged propeller blade, he told Jimmy the long story behind its development.

"These doggone propellers," he said, "have given us more headaches than any other part of the flying machine. Our experiments here with the glider last year showed Orv and me pretty much exactly how to build the machine itself. We knew how we wanted our engine built, and the only trouble there was that we had to take the time to build it ourselves. But these propellers!" He shook his head as he thought about it. "I want to tell you, Jim, they were a real pain."

"They sure don't look much like a propeller on a motorboat," Jimmy conceded.

"No, they don't. But we had to start somewhere, so we started with marine screws. Of course, it didn't take us long to find out that the kind of screw that will drive a boat through the water won't necessarily drive a flying machine through the air. For one thing, the blades are too short and wide, and they have too much pitch to them. They work all right in the water, but in the air they're just like a big, clumsy wheel. Each blade gets in the next one's way. Well, we tried two blades, three blades, and four blades, and tested them all in the wind tunnel. Then we came back to a two-blade propeller as the design that gave us the maximum thrust and driving power."

During this conversation, Orville had been tinkering with the engine for want of something better to do. Now he came over and stood beside Jimmy and Will at the workbench.

If he had a brother, Jimmy thought, he'd like him to be like the Wrights. Most brothers that he knew were all the time fighting and scrapping. But Orv and Will were more like pals than brothers. They enjoyed listening to each other talk, and were always interested in what the other one had to say. Sure, they argued and interrupted a lot. But that was good, because it made the conversation interesting, and kept it going in a lively fashion, like a baseball being tossed around the infield after a batter has been put out.

And so, true to form, Orv interrupted his brother as soon as he joined the group. But he picked up the story at precisely the point where Wilbur had left off.

"The worst headache of all," he said, "was getting just the right pitch to the blades."

Will nodded in agreement. *"That's* the truth."

"And then," Orv went on, "we finally hit it. Will got the notion that a flying machine propeller is sort of like a flying machine wing, only it goes around instead of staying in a fixed position. So in that case, it ought to be curved like a wing, instead of being a twisted flat surface like a marine screw."

Jimmy shook his head in puzzlement. If anyone had asked him, he'd have had to admit that he paid a whole lot more attention when the Wrights talked than he did when the teacher lectured in school. And when either of them said something that he didn't understand, he always asked for an explanation. He did so now.

"But don't the flying machine propeller and the boat propeller have the same purpose—to drive the boat or the machine forward?"

"Not altogether, Jim," Will said, fielding the conversational ball again. "Draw him a picture, Orv. He'll understand it easier that way."

Orv took a grimy piece of paper and a pencil stub out of his shirt pocket and spread the paper out on the bench. He drew a cross-section of the flying machine's wing.

"Now you see," he said, "the wing is fairly flat on the bottom and slightly rounded on top. And you'll also notice that, while the bow of a boat is pointed and the stern end rounded, the front edge of this wing is rounded, or blunt, and the rear edge tapers down to a point. Just the opposite from the shape of a ship that is cutting through the surface of the water."

Suddenly, Jimmy was struck by a surprising fact.

"Why, that's just how a gull's wing is shaped!"

"Sure it is," Wilbur grinned, without looking up from his work. "Or any bird's wing for that matter. But we didn't notice that important little fact until we'd tried about a hundred different wing shapes in the wind tunnel, and come up with this one."

"So the point is," Orv went on, drawing with the pencil as he talked, "when the flying machine is pushed through the air by the propellers, the air flows over the wings like this. It passes straight under the flat bottom side of the wing. But the blunt leading edge and the curved shape make the airstream bounce off the upper side of the wing in a sort of arc. Are you following me?"

"I think so," Jimmy said.

"All right. Now the curving air currents passing over the top of the wing create a vacuum. And you know the saying: 'Nature abhors a vacuum.' So the air that's *under* the wing tries to get up into the vacuum. And in that way it pushes the wing up. That's what we call lift. So if the force of this lift, or upward push, is greater than the weight of the flying machine, the machine will rise up in the air."

"Ho-ly wow!" Jimmy gasped. "So *that's* the way it works!"

"Now the propeller also helps to stir up the air currents that pass over the wing and moves the air backwards—at least we think it does—and so that's why it has to be different from a marine screw."

"Boy, oh boy!" Jimmy breathed. "They sure enough don't teach us things like that in school!"

"That's because it isn't in any books," Wilbur said drily. "Orv and I had to figure it out for ourselves. We still don't know a whole lot about it, but our wind tunnel tests seem to say we're right."

"Now I see why you have two propellers instead of one," Jim said brightly, anxious to let the Wrights know that he thoroughly understood all this complex explanation. "Two propellers give twice as much push, and twice as much breeze, as one would."

Orv shook his head.

"No, that's not quite right, Jimmy. We figure the two propellers will spread the moving air over a wider area. And then there's another thing that

we had to learn the hard way. If a propeller is spin
ning clockwise, it sets up a force that makes the
flying machine want to spin counter-clockwise.
That's Newton's Third Law—to every action
there is an equal and opposite reaction."

Somehow, Orv made Newton sound a lot more
interesting than the physics teacher ever did.

"So when you try to compensate for that coun-
ter-spin by controlling your wings and rudder,
then your propeller acts like a kind of gyroscope
and makes the machine hard to steer."

Jimmy didn't quite get this.

"But wouldn't two propellers be twice as bad?"

"It had us stumped for a long time," Orv admitted, "but we finally got the idea that if we used two propellers, spinning in opposite directions, the balance would be equalized. And, by golly, when we tried it, that's what happened."

"Will," Jimmy said—they had asked him to drop the formal "Mister" on the grounds that they were now old friends—"it seems to me that you and Orv have found out an almighty lot about flying machines that nobody else knows. With Professor Langley and Alexander Graham Bell and all those other famous people trying to build one, it would seem to me that what you've discovered ought to be worth a fortune."

Will shrugged his shoulders and snorted softly.

"Doctor Bell did a fine job when he invented the telephone, and he made a lot of money out of it too. But he doesn't know beans about flying machines."

"The trouble with those people, Jimmy boy," Orv put in, "is that they're professors and scientists and presidents of aeronautical societies—and Will and I are just a couple of country boys who never went further than high school and who run a bicycle shop for a living. So they can't see us for looking over our heads. We've written letters to most of them, explaining about our wind tunnel experiments and our new aerodynamic tables, and sometimes we get a polite note in reply and sometimes we don't. And what the notes usually say—in a nice, gentlemanly way, of course—is something like 'You little boys stick to fixing bicycles and leave the flying machines to us grown men.' So finally we decided to keep what we've learned to ourselves."

His brother's tone was growing so bitter that Will broke the spell by breaking into a sudden burst of laughter.

"Now, Orv, don't be so hard on them. I did address the Chicago Society of Engineers, didn't I?"

"That's a fact," Orv said, his face brightening. "The Society heard about our glider flights down here last winter, Jim, so they wrote and asked one of us to come to Chicago and tell the members about them. We tossed a coin, and Will went."

"I got up on the platform," Will continued, taking up the story, "and told them about our warped wings and movable rudder and all the other things we've discovered. And what do you suppose happened? After I was all through, one of the old professors came up to me and said that he had an idea for a flying machine that flew by flapping its wings, and what did I think of it? Boy, I got out of there fast. I was scared I'd lose my mind if I stuck around."

Telling the story had put Will back into a good humor again. Now he put the last finishing touches on the propeller with a piece of fine sandpaper and straightened up.

"Okay. Let's spin 'em."

They had rigged things up on the workbench so that the twin propellers were fastened to two tall frames of metal on each side of, and behind, the engine, just as they would be on the flying machine itself. Bicycle chains connected sprockets on either side of the engine to the same kind of sprockets on the propeller shafts. One of the chains was twisted into a figure eight, so that the propeller it turned would spin in an opposite direction to the other.

Now Will slipped the hub of the newly finished propeller onto its shaft and bolted it securely. He took one last look at everything, and when he was satisfied, he said:

"Let her flicker, Orv!"

Orv cranked the engine by spinning the propellers, and once more it coughed and gasped and sputtered into life. Then it settled down to a steady roar. The two propellers turned slowly at first, and then picked up speed, and finally began to spin so furiously that the individual blades disappeared, and the propellers became two shining circles of sparkling light.

A heavy piece of metal screamed past Jimmy's head

The strong windstream which they created blew the heavy clouds of exhaust smoke behind them and sent them streaming out the open door like a dark, fast-moving fog. The heavy workbench shivered and shook under the pounding vibration.

Jimmy Blair stood with his mouth open and his eyes popping at this wonderful machine which the Wrights had built. Wilbur and Orville were grinning from ear to ear, looking like proud fathers getting their first view of a newborn baby.

Jimmy could hear Orv's voice yelling over the thunderous noise: "She works, boy! She works!"

"She's a beautiful sight!" Will yelled back.

The brothers stood for a few minutes more looking at the whirling blades, as fascinated with them as Jimmy was. Then Will yelled:

"Better turn her off for now. There's no use—"

His words were cut off by a loud explosion that cracked sharply above the deafening din like the boom of a ten-gauge duck gun.

A heavy piece of metal screamed past Jimmy's head and slammed into the wall behind him. He ducked instinctively. The engine shuddered and ground to a stop. The right propeller jerked as though it had slammed into an invisible obstruction in the air—and its twin began to whirl slower and slower until it, too, was standing still.

CHAPTER NINE

The Airframe

In the first few seconds of silence, which suddenly seemed as loud as the roar of the engine had been an instant before, Jimmy and Orv and Will stood still and stared stupidly from one to the other.

"What—what happened, Will?" Orville managed at last.

The question brought Will out of his trance, and he looked around. Then he stepped over to the wall behind Jimmy and picked up a jagged piece of steel from the floor. He held it up in one hand.

"The end of the driveshaft," he said, staring at it as though it might be a poisonous snake. "There must have been a weakness in it, and it twisted right off."

He rubbed the sweat off his forehead.

"It's a good thing this missed you, Jimmy boy. It's like a slug from a Gatling gun."

Jimmy remembered the object that had whistled past his ear, and for a moment his knees became so weak that he didn't quite know whether he could trust them to hold him up. Then he gulped in two or three deep breaths, and his heart, which had been pounding like a piledriver, began to quiet down to normal.

"Gosh, Will," he gasped. "Is she ruined?"

His question went unanswered, for Will and Orv had immediately leaped to the workbench to find the answer for themselves.

For the next fifteen or twenty minutes, nothing was said except short mutterings and half-sentences as the brothers patiently went over every part of the engine, the shafts, and the propellers. At last, Will turned away from the bench and breathed a deep sigh of relief.

"Orv, we're the luckiest guys in the United States. I thought the insides had been ripped clean out of that engine, and all the running gear put on the blink too. But except for being jarred out of kilter, the only real damage is this shaft."

"That's damage enough, Will." Orv shook his head and scratched at his unruly shock of hair. "I don't know where in the world we're going to get a replacement."

"There's only one place in the world, kiddo. And I don't like to think about it. I'm going to have to take this all the way back to Dayton and help Charley make a new one."

"Who's Charley?" Jimmy asked.

"He's our mechanic in the shop back home," Orv told him. "He did most of the machine work on this engine, and he's the only machinist we can trust to turn out this new shaft. But, Will," he said, turning to his brother, "I think I ought to be the one to make this trip. I worked with Charley on the engine more than you did. And while I'm gone, you and Jim can start putting the machine together."

"No, you don't, little brother!" Will said, smiling for the first time since the accident. "That trip will be no picnic." He reached into his pocket and pulled out a coin. "I'll toss you for it, Orv. Call it."

"Heads."

Will spun the coin in the air, and when it landed in his palm it was heads.

"All right, you win," Will grinned. "Give my regards to the folks."

"Can I get a boat to the mainland tonight, Jim?" Orv asked.

"Wouldn't be much point if you could," Jim replied. "There's no train north till tomorrow noon. But tomorrow's Saturday, and no school, so I'll come out early with the buckboard."

He smiled as a vagrant thought wandered into his head.

"It's too bad the flying machine isn't working. If it was, you could just fly up to Ohio and get what you want and fly back."

"Whoa up!" Orville said, grinning. "I'm afraid it will be a long time before flying machines are carrying passengers and baggage like the railway cars."

"I don't know, Orv," Will reminded him. "You said yourself that if a machine had enough power and the proper wingspread, there'd be no limit to the load it could lift."

Orv aimed a mock jab at Jimmy's head.

"Anyway, Jim, as they say down here in Carolina, you're a good boy, sure enough."

After Orville had gone, Wilbur spent two or three days puttering with the engine, tightening it up where the shock of the breaking shaft had loosened nuts and bolts and thrown delicate parts out of adjustment. Miraculously, the accident had done no damage to the propeller chain, and soon, except for the missing driveshaft, the whole thing was in good order again.

"We might as well get started on the airframe, Jim," Will said one afternoon.

"The airframe?" Jimmy asked. This was a word he hadn't heard before.

"The body of the flying machine—the wings and the rudders," Will told him. "Orv started calling it that, for want of a better word, to distinguish it from the engine and the propellers. But it's going to be mighty slow work without Orv here to help us."

When he looked at all the pieces that had been so carefully prefabricated in Dayton, Jimmy couldn't make head nor tail of them. They looked like the parts of a giant jigsaw puzzle, except that all the pieces seemed to be the same.

Will was right about it being slow work. By the end of the day, they hadn't quite finished one of the lower wing sections. Jimmy realized that he was of little or no help at all. The only thing he could do was hand Will a particular piece after it had been pointed out to him, and then hold it while Will bolted it into place.

Finally, looking up, Will's eyes lit on the old glider that hung suspended from the rafters.

"Jim," he said, "there isn't much use trying to hurry things, under the circumstances. Haste makes waste, Pa always used to tell Orv and me. If it's a nice day tomorrow, why don't we take the glider out and make a few practice flights? I'll need to keep my hand in if I expect to be able to handle the flying machine when we're ready to try her out."

When Jim arrived at the camp the next day, Will had already taken down the glider, cleaned it up, and tightened all the struts and bracing wires. Now it stood on the sand in front of the shack.

"I've figured out a way for one man to launch her," he said. "I tied a square L-hook to the end of the launching rope. Then we put the hook behind the runner-brace. As long as you keep the rope taut, the hook will hold and you can pull me off the top of the dune. But once the rope slackens, the hook will fall free. What say we try it?"

Jimmy didn't need an invitation for any such sport as this, so they carried the glider to the top of Kill Devil Hill from where she had been launched so many times last year.

When they had it poised on the brink of the hill, ready to catch the first brisk gust of wind, Will stretched out prone on the lower wing and took the controls in his hands. Jimmy backed halfway down the slope, keeping the L-hook tight. The wind freshened against his back, and a second later he heard Will's "Go!"

Jimmy pulled hard, but steady, on the tow-rope, and the glider took off like a kite. The square hook freed itself and fell to the sand, and the glider whizzed over Jimmy's head. He could hear the wind whipping the muslin covering of the wings, and see Will shifting his body as he manipulated the controls. The glider rose up on the waves of air, like a dory riding a swell, and then it swooped down, leveled off, and came to rest on the sand, a

hundred yards away, as lightly as a swallow landing on the branch of a sweet-gum tree.

Will made two or three more flights in this manner, and then Jimmy said:

"How about me next, Will?"

"I don't know," Will said. "I don't know what your pa would say."

"He said it was okay when I flew her last year," Jimmy begged.

"That's a fact," Will conceded, "so I guess he won't mind." Then he grinned. "But if you hurt yourself, I'm going to skedaddle out of Kitty Hawk a lot faster than any flying machine could take me."

For a year, Jimmy had thought of nothing but his brief moment of free flight last fall. But the instant Will pulled the tow rope and jerked him free of the earth, it was as though the intervening year had never happened—as though he had been up here riding the air waves ever since.

The breeze he was floating on top of was a particularly stiff one, and he had to keep his mind on the controls at all times. He was careful not to fight them, but instead to ease them and baby them as he did the tiller of a sailboat, letting the airstream carry him along instead of trying to buck it.

And because the breeze was stiff and steady, it carried him higher than the glider had ever soared before—nearly fifty feet, he judged, by the size of Will's tiny figure 'way down there on the sand.

As he planed down, he kept the nose-rudder high, then leveled off until the runners skidded across the sand.

In a minute, Will came running up, his face wreathed in a big smile.

"Jim, you're a natural born flyer! I swear, boy! You've only ridden that thing twice, and both times you've beat the tar out of me and Orv. We're going to have to take some flying lessons from you before we tackle the power machine!"

During the month of October, while they waited for Orville to return with the new shaft, Jim and Will worked every day on the airframe. But without Orv's help, the job crept along like a crippled snail. Jimmy worked hard and did the best he could, but he knew that he was a poor substitute for Orv.

Orville had originally figured on taking two weeks to make the trip to Dayton, cut and machine the new part, and return to North Carolina. But telegrams from him explained the delay.

The original shaft had been made of a length

of tubing. After arriving in Dayton, Orv and Charley had talked it over and decided that they had better play it safe and make the replacement of solid steel. Then, a week later, came another wire. As long as they were making the main drive-shaft of solid steel, they thought they might as well make new steel shafts for the propellers.

And so the original two weeks lengthened out into better than four. Day by day, the airframe of the flying machine took shape. And whenever the weather and the wind were especially good, Will and Jimmy spent at least a couple of hours making practice flights in the glider. They got so good that they could twist it and turn it and make it soar around in half circles.

"Boy, oh boy!" Will said one day. "Just think what we can do with our flying machine when we've got an engine on her to give her power!"

When Orv returned to Kitty Hawk during the first week of November with the new steel shafts, the pace of the work speeded up. It took less than a day to put the engine and propeller gear in shape, and this time they ran as smoothly as the works of a good clock.

With Orville back on the job, the airframe was completed in jig-time. Clara came out to the camp and spent two afternoons sewing the muslin wing-covering. Wilbur and Orville, with Jimmy helping, installed the engine on the rear of the lower wing, and rigged the twin propellers on either side and behind it.

And there, one day—suddenly, as though a genie had jumped out of a magic lamp and waved his wand—there stood the flying machine! There stood the mechanical bird that the Wrights had dreamed about, and sweated over, and spent all their spare money on for the last five years! There stood the answer to all the scientists and the professors and the wise old men who had said that man would never fly. There she stood, all ready to try her shiny new muslin wings.

And she was a wonderful sight to behold. Nothing like her had ever been built in all the history of the world. Her wings were forty feet from tip to tip, so wide that the Wrights would have to turn her sideways to get her out of the shack. She had a vertical rudder behind, and a horizontal rudder up front. And her two propellers on either side of the engine looked as dainty and jaunty as the ostrich plumes on a lady's hat.

"Will," Orv said in a solemn voice, after the last screw and the last bolt had been put in place, "sometimes I thought we'd never see her, all in one piece like this. But there she is at last, and she's worth every minute and every dollar we've put into her."

"Hold your horses, little brother," Will said. "You're only seeing her on the ground. Save the national anthem till you see her in the air."

"Let's try her tomorrow, Will," Orville said, his eyes shining like those of a small boy who has just heard that the circus is coming to town.

"We've got a lot of things to do before we try her in the air," Will said. Then he gave his brother a shove that almost knocked him off balance. "But don't worry, kiddo. I'm as anxious to see her fly as you are."

"So am I," said Jimmy Blair.

At that moment Clara came bursting through the door of the shack. Her face was flushed, and she was panting hard as though she had been running.

"Jimmy—Mr. Wright—the man from the government weather station—says that a big storm—is blowing up. He says to—to tie everything down!"

Wilbur groaned.

"Oh, great balls of fire! This is just what we need! Come on, boys! Let's batten down the hatches!"

CHAPTER TEN

Bad Luck Blows In

THEY had been so engrossed in admiring the flying machine that neither Jimmy nor the Wrights had noticed the storm making up outside. Now, looking out over the dunes in the direction of the Atlantic, they could see heavy black clouds scudding across the sky before the angry wind. Bits of brush and pieces of paper skittered across the sand like frightened land crabs, and the sand itself rattled against the walls of the shack like hailstones.

"Get on my bike, Clara," Jimmy ordered, "and skedaddle for home before the rainstorm hits. Tell Mama I'm going to stay here and help Will and Orv."

Clara climbed onto the bicycle as Jimmy held it for her, the cross-bar bunching up her long skirts and revealing a modest length of cotton stocking above high-button shoes. Jimmy steadied the wheel for her and then gave her a shove. With her little feet pumping furiously and her long hair whipping behind her in the wind, she raced down the sandy road.

Jimmy watched her until she disappeared out of sight around a dune, then he re-entered the shack. The Wrights were hurridly hauling out coils of rope with which to secure the flying machine.

"Let the door down, Jim," Will yelled over his shoulder.

Jimmy removed the poles that propped up the front wall of the shack, lowered it into place and made it fast. Then he closed and latched a smaller door in the adjoining wall. This done, he jumped to help Will and Orv tie down the flying machine.

As he worked, he kept mental track of the time. When he estimated that half an hour had gone by, he breathed easier. Clara would be safe at home by now.

Racing against time and the howling wind that was blowing harder with every gust, they tied lengths of rope to struts, runners, rudders, and every available projection on the airframe, and lashed them securely to the walls, the rafters, the workbench, and the floor. When they were through, the big flying machine looked like Gulliver after he had been captured in his sleep and tied down by the Lilliputians.

"Well," Orv said at last, "that ought to hold her —unless the shack blows in."

He had no sooner spoken than a fresh gust hit them, driving before it a solid sheet of rain. Through the shack's single window, Jim could see flashes of lightning split the sky, followed by booming blasts of thunder. The thin walls of the frail building shivered and quaked, and the flying machine, tied down as it was, shook and danced against the securing lines like a nervous horse.

The rain had blotted out the late afternoon sun, and through the window the outdoors was as dark as night. Will and Orv hovered around the machine like mother hens around a single chick, as though to hold it down themselves if worst should come to worst.

For an hour the storm pounded on the shack

with its full fury. Water seeped in through cracks in the walls and partially covered the floor.

Suddenly, with a crack like a pistol shot, the latch on the small door snapped and the door slammed inward and banged against the wall. A sheet of icy rain water spilled in through the open doorway as though some angry giant had flung the contents of a giant pail. By the time Will, Orv, and Jimmy managed to get the door closed again and propped shut with a length of two-by-four, all three were soaking, shivering wet.

Orv lit the alcohol cookstove, and now the three of them huddled around it in a feeble effort to absorb some of the heat from its hissing flame. As they hunched over the fire, the Wrights kept constantly looking around the shack, alert for the first sign of a new danger.

It wasn't long in coming. Another furious blast of wind rattled the shack, and with it came a crash overhead and a sharp ripping sound.

"The roof!" Will yelled. "The tarpaper's ripping off!"

Orv ran to the workbench and scooped up a handful of nails and a hammer.

"Help me with this ladder!" he roared.

Jimmy was at his side in an instant, and between the two of them they picked up a long ladder that lay on the floor against the wall. When they were ready, Will opened the door and they plunged out into the full force of the wind-driven, ice-cold rain. Will closed the door behind them from the inside.

Once out in the open, the wind caught them and sent them staggering around helplessly in the darkness. After two or three tries, they managed to lean the ladder against the wall of the shack and, with Jimmy holding it at the bottom, Orv started climbing. When he was halfway up, a freak wind current whipped around the side of the shack and knocked the ladder backward as sharply as if it had been struck by a battering ram.

Jimmy sidestepped out of its way, slipped, and fell. Orv jumped backward, and when he hit the wet, slimy sand, he rolled sideways. A split second later the heavy ladder thudded into the ground where his body had been.

With the wind howling and shrieking in their ears like a pack of crazy banshees, and the stinging rain whipping into their faces without mercy, Orv and Jimmy tried again. This time Orv managed to get to the roof's eave.

The job required a man with four hands—one to hold onto the ladder, one to grab the flapping strips of tarpaper, one to hold the nails, and a fourth to manipulate the hammer. Even then, it would have been almost impossible. Since Orv was equipped with only the normal human number of two hands, it was completely hopeless. But somehow he managed to capture some of the truant pieces of roofing and nail them back to the wood.

The ladder was fighting Jimmy like a mad bull. In five minutes, his arms and back were aching from the effort to keep it upright; to keep it from sliding off to one side or the other, or from toppling backwards as it had on the first try. In fifteen minutes, every muscle in his body was screaming in agony, even though the icy rain was having a numbing effect.

At the end of a half hour, he was sure he couldn't stand the torture for another second. And then he noticed that the noise of the wind and the fury of the rain seemed to be abating. Orv must have noticed the same thing, for at that moment he came clambering down the ladder's rungs.

"It's letting up, Jim," he yelled in the boy's ears. "Let's go back inside before we drown or freeze to death."

Will answered their loud pounding on the door and let them in.

"Sorry I couldn't come out and help you, boys," he said, "but I figured I ought to stay in here and look after the machine."

Both Orv and Jimmy looked in the direction of the flying machine the instant their eyes became adjusted to the dim light cast by the stove and the oil lamp Will had lighted. Aside from the fact that most of her wing-covering was wet, she didn't look any the worse for her experience. Jimmy stepped over and patted her affectionately.

"It's slackening up, Will," Orv announced.

"I could tell that from in here. I was just getting ready to come out and get you when you knocked on the door."

Water was pouring into the shack from the part of the roof where the tarpaper had ripped away, but compared to the windy darkness outside, it was as snug as Mrs. Blair's kitchen.

Orville went to the stove. "I could use a hot cup of coffee," he announced through chattering teeth and blue lips. "You want me to fix you some Postum, Will?"

"Tonight," Will replied, "I'll have my coffee straight, and about triple strength if you please."

By the time they sat down to the table with their steaming cups in their hands, the wind had died down to a low, steady growl. And the sheets of rain that had been splashing against the shack's walls dwindled to a moderate dripping.

"We're used to these storms," Jimmy said. "We have them every fall. They blow up fast, whip the peninsula like they're dead set on washing the whole thing clean out to sea, and then peter out about as fast as they come in. This will be all cleared up by morning."

"All the same, I'm just about tuckered out," Orv said when the coffee pot was empty. "Let's see if we can find some dry clothes and blankets, and then all try to catch a little shut-eye."

From a trunk he extracted three shirts, three pairs of trousers and a couple of towels. They stripped off their wet clothes, rubbed themselves briskly, and got into the dry ones. Then Orv found some blankets that were only slightly damp.

Jimmy cleared a space on the workbench and climbed up. He wrapped the blanket around him and used a rolled-up tool kit as a pillow. He started to say good night, but before his lips could form the words, he was sound asleep.

By morning, as Jimmy predicted, the storm had blown itself out, but the weather was far from being cleared up. A soggy mist dripped out of a leaden sky, and the winds that blew across the dunes were clammy and bone-chilling cold.

"I'd better get on home," Jimmy suggested. "The folks will be anxious about me."

"You do that, Jimmy," Will said. "You don't

want your ma to worry." He looked around at the shambles the storm had made of the shack. "It looks like Orv and I are going to have our hands full here."

Taking the shortcut over the top of Kill Devil Hill, Jimmy looked down toward the water's edge. A large fishing boat had broken loose from its mooring lines and been washed up on the beach. The force of the wind and waves had apparently capsized it and rolled it over and over like a log, for now it lay a good fifty feet from the edge of the breakers, and its propeller jutted up grotesquely into the air. A dozen men were working around it, cutting away the tangle of lines and making preparations to right it. Jimmy would have liked to go down and watch them for a while, but he made himself resist the temptation, and went on toward home.

When he walked in the front gate, he saw that aside from a few broken branches strewn around the yard there had been no damage. The family was sitting around the table, just finishing breakfast.

His mother leaped up and threw her arms around him.

"Oh, Jimmy! Jimmy!" she almost sobbed. "We were nearly distracted about you, son."

His father wore a huge smile of relief on his craggy face, but all he said was: "Now, Lucy! I told you the boy could take care of himself."

He reached out and touched Jimmy's sleeve.

"But you'd better shuck out of those wet clothes before you catch your death."

When Jimmy had changed and come back to the kitchen, a heaping plate of hot breakfast was waiting for him. At the good smell of it, he realized how ravenously hungry he was, and he began to wolf it down. As he ate, he was besieged by a barrage of questions.

Between mouthfuls of eggs and grits and hot biscuits, he tried to answer them. After he had told the full story of the adventures in the shack, he mentioned the fishing boat he had seen below Kill Devil Hill.

"That makes six boat wrecks altogether, then," his father said. "One of the men from the weather station drove by this morning, and he said five others had washed up last night."

"The storm was rotten luck for Will and Orv," Jimmy said. "The flying machine is all finished, and they were going to try her today or tomorrow."

"I'm afraid the storm blew your flying friends a heap of bad luck. The station man said this weather has set in for at least a week or two."

CHAPTER ELEVEN

The Long Wait

THE week or two of bad weather that the man from the station had predicted stretched out into three weeks, and then four. Will and Orville fumed and fretted at the delay, and Jimmy fretted with them.

They repaired the shack and made it weatherproof again. They went over every detail of the flying machine with a fine-tooth comb—every bolt, every wire, every seam. They had decided that the machine would have a better chance of getting into the air if it took off from a smooth surface instead of the soft sand. So they built a sixty-foot monorail of hard wood which they covered with sheet metal. This they polished and greased.

It was now well into December. The brothers had been at Kitty Hawk for more than two months.

Finally, Orv couldn't stand it any longer.

"Look, Will," he said earnestly. "Let's try her anyway. At least we'll get an idea of whether she's going to fly or not."

Will shook his head.

"No, little brother. We've worked too hard and we've come too far and we've got too much at stake to take any chances we don't have to. You read in the paper what happened to Professor Langley the other day."

"What was that?" Jimmy asked. "I must have missed it."

"Well, you know that the government has spent a pile of money financing Langley's machine. He called it an aerodrome. So a couple of days ago he announced that it was all ready to fly. They launched it off a houseboat in the Potomac River,

and the contraption went over the side like a rock and hit the water. The man who was riding it was nearly drowned."

"Shucks!" Orv snorted. "We've known all along that Langley's theories were cockeyed. Our wind tunnel tests proved it."

"Just the same," Will said firmly, "I don't want it officially declared that the Wrights are cockeyed too. When we try it, I want every advantage we can get, including good weather. And if we don't get it this fall, we'll find some kind of warehouse in town to store the machine, and come back and try her in the spring."

On a Tuesday morning, a few days after Wilbur's decision to wait out the weather, Jimmy woke up to a bright sun shining through his window out of an almost cloudless sky. He jumped into his clothes, ran downstairs and out into the yard. The weather was perfect.

His mother called from the kitchen. "Hurry and eat your breakfast, Jimmy, or you'll be late for school."

Jimmy fidgeted through his classes, not hearing a word his teachers were saying. He could think only of the bright sun shining outside, and of the eager preparations the Wrights must be making right at that moment to get their flying machine into the air. He remembered his Sunday School teacher saying once that all prayers are answered when the heart is pure. Hoping fervently that his own heart was pure enough to pass the test, he prayed as hard as he could that Will and Orv wouldn't try it till he got there.

When the bell rang ending the last class of the day, he raced out of the building, climbed on his bike, and pumped furiously for the camp.

When he pulled up, breathless, in front of the shack, the Wrights had trundled out the flying machine. Now it stood on the sand, its wings gleaming in the sun. Both Will and Orv wore grins as wide as their faces, as they fiddled around it making last-minute adjustments.

"How do you like this weather, Jim?" Orv called, his voice vibrant with excitement.

"Are we going to try her today?" Jimmy asked.

"Nope," Will said. "I talked to the weather station people this morning. The winds today and tomorrow are expected to be extremely light. And we need a good twenty-mile breeze to be sure of the best results. If their figures are correct, we'll have ideal conditions on Thursday. So we plan to ground-test her this afternoon and tomorrow, and then fly her on Thursday morning."

Jimmy groaned, and suddenly almost burst into tears.

"Thursday *morning?* Oh, my gosh! I'll be in school then!"

"We thought about that, Jim," Orv said. "If anybody deserves to be here when she flies, it's you, and that's for dead certain sure." He scratched his long chin as though he didn't quite know how to go on. "But, shucks, Jim! You know how it is. If we have a good breeze in the morning —and we wait till afternoon—and the breeze dies down—"

All at once Jimmy's face brightened into a smile.

"Don't you fret, Orv," he grinned. "I've played hookey before, and I guess I can play it again. And I'll tell you one thing. All the wild horses on Chincoteague Island couldn't keep me away from here Thursday morning!"

Convincing his father had been no problem at all, and so the next day in school Jimmy presented a folded piece of paper to his teacher.

"This is an excuse from my father, Mr. Kane. I won't be in classes tomorrow."

The teacher made a clucking noise with his tongue.

"Dear me!" he said. "I trust nothing has gone wrong at home."

"Oh, no," Jimmy assured him. "But, you see, I've been working with Orville and Wilbur Wright out at Kill Devil Hill, helping them build their flying machine. They're going to try her out tomorrow morning, and Papa says I can be there to watch."

Mr. Kane's face darkened, but Jimmy didn't notice it as he rambled on, his enthusiasm mounting.

"Why don't you take the whole class out, sir? It will be a real historic—"

"Poppycock!" the teacher exploded. "I should think your father would be more concerned with your school marks than in having you hang around a pair of crazy inventors with tomfool ideas about flying. Any idiot knows that an airship can't fly without a gasbag. I've explained that in class a dozen times."

Jimmy was surprised by Mr. Kane's sudden outburst, but he said loyally:

"The Wrights' machine will fly, sir. Why even I have flown in their big glider!"

The teacher shook his head at the idea of such nonsense.

"Well," he said at last, "there's nothing I can do about this excuse. But I am certainly not going to dismiss the whole class just so it can go on an idiotic wild goose chase. And you, young man," he added dourly, "had better be sure you know tomorrow's lessons by heart when I see you again on Friday."

CHAPTER TWELVE

The First Flight

JIMMY arrived at camp the next morning, long before the sun. He had slept fitfully, waking up a dozen times to creep down to the kitchen for a look at the clock. Finally, he gave up sleep as a bad job, and got dressed. There was not a light nor a sound on the Blair place when he went out to the stable to get his bike.

But early as he was, the Wrights had been even earlier. The oil lamp was throwing its feeble rays out the big door when he pulled up and leaned his wheel against the shack.

Orville was pouring coffee. "Well, Jim," he said brightly, "couldn't you sleep either?"

"Not a wink," Jimmy grinned.

"Want a cup of coffee?"

"Mama thinks I'm too young to drink coffee. But I like it, and a cup sure would go good."

"I'm not usually a coffee drinker either." Will smiled. "But this is the big day, so I allow we've got a right to celebrate."

He took a sip, then put his cup down on the table with a nervous gesture.

"I wonder how the wind's doing?"

He got up and went out the door, and when he came back he was grinning.

"She's just fine," he reported. "Nice and brisk and steady. Just fine."

Orville was grinning foolishly too, and Jimmy found himself doing the same thing. Everyone was in a wonderfully exhilarated mood, and there seemed to be an electric charge sparking the air, on this Thursday morning of December 17, 1903.

When they had finished their coffee and Jimmy had cleared away the cups, Will said:

"First, let's move the flying machine outside. Then we'll give the engine one final go."

It was full light by the time they tenderly trundled the big machine out to the strip of sand in front of the shack. The pale rays of the rising sun, shining down through the hazy air, tinted her sleek wings a light shade of pink.

Orv took one last look at the engine and primed it.

"All right," he said, "let her flicker!"

147

Will cranked the engine by turning over the propellers. Gradually it coughed into action, and then settled down to a steady, deep-throated roar, the spinning propellers throwing a stiff slipstream of air behind them that stirred up the sand like a miniature cyclone.

"Easy, Will," Orv cautioned. "Not too much speed."

Will throttled down, and the blades spun with a humming whine that could be heard over the racket of the engine.

Orv signaled with his hand, and his brother cut the engine.

"Now," Will said, when the propellers had slowed to a stop and the flying machine stood once more lifeless on the sand, "let's rig up the launching rail."

They carried the rail in sections about 100 ft. north of the building, and stretched it out in a straight line. They bolted the sections together, and at last had a smooth, shining, sixty-foot length of rail down along which the flying machine could roll to its take-off point.

It was nearly ten by Orv's gold watch, and they were getting ready to start the engine, when the first visitors arrived.

"I passed the word around the village that we

were going to try her this morning," Will told Jimmy, "and invited anybody who was interested to come on out and watch."

"That's Mr. Etheridge, Mr. Dough, and Mr. Daniels from the Government Life Saving Station," Jimmy said.

The three men waved a greeting.

"Need any help with that thing?"

"Sure," Will called back. "We can always use an extra hand."

The three men approached the flying machine gingerly, as though the touch of their hands might damage the odd-looking craft. But under Will's direction, they helped move the machine along the sand and soon had it perched on the rail.

And the world's first manmade bird sat poised for flight.

"You think that thing will fly?" one of the men asked nervously.

"We sure hope so!" Orv replied, half laughing, half serious.

Just then Rock came trotting around the base of the hill, pulling the Blair family buckboard. Jimmy's father and mother and a stranger were on the seat. Clara stood up in the back, holding on. Jim breathed a deep sigh of relief. He'd been afraid they might not get here in time.

Mr. Blair and the stranger climbed down.

"This is Mr. Brinkley, from over Manteo way," Jimmy's father said. "He was in town on business, and thought he'd come out and see the fun."

"You're all certainly most welcome," Wilbur said. "Would you like to look over the flying machine?"

Standing behind it, the seven visitors peered curiously at the Wrights' creation, but they stood at a respectful distance, as though fearful of getting too close to this strange beast of the air.

Now a few clouds had gathered in the sky, and the sun hid its brilliance behind them. The wind freshened and suddenly became cooler. Will and Orv looked apprehensively up at the gray sky, a worried look on their faces for the first time that day.

"It's half after ten, Orv," Wilbur said. "I think we're ready."

"As ready as we'll ever be," Orv replied. "Climb on. You go first."

"Nothing doing, little brother!" Will said in a soft voice. "We're going to make it. I know that as well as I know I'm standing here. And whoever rides that wing will have the honor of going down in history as the first man who ever flew. You want it to be me, and I want it to be you. So—"

Grinning, he reached into his pocket for a coin.

"Call it!"

"Heads!"

The silver coin glittered in the air, and came down heads.

Will touched Orville on the shoulder.

"God bless you, kiddo!"

Briefly, the brothers shook hands, and then Orv crawled onto the lower wing and lay down flat, his hands grasping the controls. He lay to the left of the engine, with the propellers behind him on either side.

Will stepped over to make sure that everything was all set, then he went back to the right side of the machine.

Jimmy took a last look up into the sky. Half a dozen gulls and fish hawks were soaring around in smooth, effortless circles.

"Look out, you up there!" His mind didn't consciously form the words or even the complete thought. But just the same it was there, unspoken, somewhere in the back of his head. "This is the last day you'll ever have that big sky all to yourselves!"

Suddenly the coughing and spitting of the engine blasted him out of his reverie. He glued his eyes to the prone figure of Orville. The engine settled down into a steady, drumming roar. Black clouds of smoke streamed back from it and stung

Jimmy's eyes. But he didn't dare blink them even once.

The propellers were spinning furiously. Orv advanced the throttle, and they whirled so rapidly that they became a blur, and the windstream they threw out behind them whipped Jim's hair and pounded into his face. The muslin covering of the wings flapped and fluttered and then, as the speed of the propellers increased, became taut. The whole flying machine quivered and shook, as though struggling to free itself from the earth that held it captive.

When the roar of the engine reached an ear-splitting crescendo, Will took a firm hold of the wing-tip to steady the flying machine when it started.

Orville tripped the releasing trigger, and the machine started along the monorail, Will running at its side. Twenty feet. Thirty feet. Forty feet. And then—

She lifted into the air!

She climbed to a height of about ten feet, and then dipped down. Orv brought her front rudder up, and she swooped upward again.

At the height of her climb—about twelve feet off the ground—she dipped down again, and her runners skidded across the sand some hundred feet beyond the end of the launching rail!

There was an instant of silence on the hill behind him, and then the little group of people who had been watching broke out into a screaming cheer. Jim found himself cheering and yelling along with the rest. The men from the Life-Saving Station ran past him, and he joined them.

When they came to the flying machine, her engine now quiet and her propellers still, Orv had climbed out from the wing, and Will had thrown his arms around him in a big bear hug as the brothers thumped each other on the back.

"She flies, Orv! She flies!"

Orv disengaged himself as Jim and the Life-Saving men rushed up.

"She sure does," Orv said, his face flushed with excitement and his white teeth bared in a big grin of triumph. "But I should have kept her up when she dipped down that last time."

"Forget it, kid!" Will said happily. "How high you flew and how far you went doesn't matter. We'll do better next time. The important thing is that you got her off the ground. We know she can fly! I timed you at twelve seconds. And that's just twelve seconds longer than anybody ever flew before!"

Suddenly Will, who usually tried to keep his

dignity, went crazy. He took off his cap and tossed it into the air.

"Yippee!" he yelled, screaming like a wild Indian. "Yippee! We made it!"

When the initial excitement had died down to a somewhat bewildered acceptance of the fact that a powered flying machine had at long last flown through the air, and that these people who had come out to Kill Devil Hill this morning had seen it with their own eyes, Orv said:

"Let's take her back and try her again."

The men from the Life-Saving Station eagerly

bent to the task of pulling the machine back to its starting point. And Jimmy was a little surprised to see that his father and Mr. Brinkley were also helping.

Clara and his mother were standing by the track. They hadn't moved since the machine started its flight.

Now Clara ran over and grasped Jimmy by the arm.

"Isn't it wonderful, Jim? The Wrights said it would fly—and it does!"

"And a lot of credit goes to you, young lady!"

Orville Wright had suddenly appeared at their side. "You sewed the wings, don't forget that. And she couldn't have flown without them."

This time Will lay down on the wing, and Orville gave the signal. The engine roared. The propellers whirred. Jimmy released the catch as before.

The flying machine shot along the rail and into the air. For an instant it wobbled, and Will straightened it out. It flew on a little farther than Orv had been able to take it.

They made a third flight, with Orv again at the controls, and he bettered Wilbur's distance by ten feet.

Once more, willing hands pulled the machine back to the launching rail.

"What do you say we go once more before we call it a day?" Will asked.

"I say it's the biggest day of our lives, so we might as well make it as big as we can."

Will got into position, and as he did so, Jimmy heard Orv say:

"Look here, boy. Everything we do today is a record. So why don't you give them a real good one to shoot at?"

Will nodded and started the engine. Orville

stepped back as the propellers began to whirl. When they were going full speed, Orv gave the signal and Jim released the catch.

For the fourth time that day, the flying machine lifted into the air. But this time it didn't seem as if it was ever coming down. Trailing smoke and spurts of flame from the engine, it flew on and on, keeping steadfastly at about the same height above the ground. Then the right wing went down, and Will straightened it up. He must have over-controlled a little, for immediately the left wing heeled over. Again Will straightened the machine out on a level course, and it kept flying on until it looked no bigger than a gull. Then it dipped down and came to rest on the sand.

Never in all his life had Jimmy heard such a shouting and yelling as came from the men who were watching. With one impulse, they started running toward the distant flying machine.

When they reached it, Will had already climbed out and was jogging toward them. Orv was the first to reach him.

"Boy, oh boy!" he screamed, almost knocking his brother down in his wild enthusiasm. "I said make a record, and you made one! I timed you at fifty-nine seconds! Just short of a full minute!"

Mr. Daniels, from the Life-Saving Station, was shouting to be heard over the din:

"Part of my job at the station is estimating distances. And I'd say you made better than eight hundred and fifty feet!"

"Will," Orv yelled over the hubbub of excited voices, "I'd say we've had a good day. Let's quit while we're ahead!"

It was unusual for roast turkey to be on the Blair table except at Thanksgiving and Christmas. But supper tonight was a celebration, and the big gobbler that Mrs. Blair had been fattening up for Christmas Day was the center of attraction.

The meal had been a happy one, with everybody around the table—Will, Orv, Clara, Jimmy, and Mr. and Mrs. Blair—all talking at once about the wondrous events of the day. Even Jimmy's father, who only a short time before had dismissed flying machines as tomfoolery, was infected by what he had seen that morning by Kill Devil Hill.

At last, with the turkey reduced to a framework of bones, everyone seemed to be momentarily talked out, content to sit back and enjoy the feeling of having been well fed.

Now, Jimmy thought to himself, is the time!

"Will," he said, "I don't ever want to do anything in my life but build and fly flying machines.

It didn't seem as if it was ever coming down

Going to school won't do me a bit of good, because all they teach you is that flying is impossible."

He paused for a second, but no one said anything so he took the plunge.

"Look, Will—Orv—take me back to Ohio with you! You can teach me about flying machines, and nobody else can. I'll do any kind of work you want done—" His eyes were pleading and he raced on. "I'll sweep out your shop, I'll run your errands—"

"Wait a minute, Jim," Wilbur drawled, choosing his words carefully. "What we did today is only a beginning, and a mighty puny little beginning at that. Sure—we proved that a flying machine can get off the ground. But staying in the air for fifty-nine seconds, and covering a total distance of eight hundred and fifty-two feet, is of no practical use at all. We've got a long road ahead of us, and it isn't going to be easy. To begin with, Orv and I are flat broke. We've spent every dollar we had."

He stopped, as if to gather his thoughts.

"What we've got to do now is go back to work and build a better flying machine—one that can fly high, and go fast, and stay off the ground for long periods of time. Nobody knows how long that's going to take. Least of all, Orv and me. But I'll tell you what I'll do, Jim. I'll make you a proposition."

Jimmy straightened in his chair and leaned forward, as though he was scared he wouldn't hear every word that Will was about to say.

"The one big handicap that Orv and I have had to overcome has been our lack of a technical education. We've always had to figure things out the hard way. But if flying machines are ever going to amount to anything, they're going to need trained engineers to build them. So here's my proposition. You finish high school, and then you go on to college and study engineering. And if by that time Orv and I have been able to prove that flight in heavier-than-air machines is really practical, Mr. James Blair, college graduate, will be hired as Chief Engineer of the Wright Flying Machine Company."

He grinned and stuck out his hand.

"Is that a deal, Jim?"

"That's a deal, Will," Jimmy said, and his eyes were shining as though he was seeing a far-off vision. "That's a deal for doggone certain!"

CHAPTER THIRTEEN

The Army Contract

1908

JIMMY Blair stood by the open window of his dormitory room, gazing out at the campus of North Carolina University and turning a letter over and over in his hands. He was not looking at the oaks and elms and maples that lined the quiet campus walks. Instead, his mind was racing back over the past four and a half years.

Through occasional items that had appeared in the newspapers, and more frequent letters from Will and Orv, he had followed the Wrights' fortunes as closely as he could. And the fortunes had mostly been misfortunes.

In one newspaper story, which carried a Washington dateline, the writer had asked: "Are the Wrights flyers or liars?"

The letters had been more informative.

Back in Dayton, in the spring of 1904, Will and Orv had built a bigger and better flying machine.

After testing it successfully in a farmer's pasture field, they invited the people of the town out for an exhibition. The engine failed, and the people laughed. This experience, Orv wrote, made them decide to put on no more public shows, but instead to do their experimental work in private.

Before the end of the year, they had flown as far as four miles, staying in the air over five minutes. A year later, in the fall of 1905, they had made two continuous flights of more than twenty miles.

It was at this point, one of the letters said, that they had tried to interest the United States Army in buying a Wright flying machine, or *Flyer* as they were now calling it, for use in observation. "But the War Department," Orv wrote, "persists in believing that there is no such thing as a flying machine, even though the Associated Press carried a story about our latest twenty-four-mile flight."

Jimmy had read the AP story, and he wondered what kind of fatheads they had in the War Department.

But this letter he had received today was like a bright ray of sunshine stabbing through the gloom.

"President Theodore Roosevelt saw an article about our *Flyer* in *Scientific American* last fall," the letter read in part, "and he lit a fire under the

Army. Now they have agreed to buy one or more machines from us at $25,000 each, if the *Flyer* can carry two men, fly for an hour at an average speed of forty mph., carry enough fuel for a 125-mile flight, and be transported in Army wagons. We can do it, Jim. We'll be making our first trial flight with a passenger at Kitty Hawk on or about May 14. Can you be there?"

Could he be there? He'd like to see anybody try to keep him away! He stuck the letter in his coat pocket and went to see the Dean.

Jimmy had changed a lot since the Wrights had seen him last. He was a little better than six feet tall now, and his arms and shoulders had filled out to man's size. He was determined to be a good engineer—the first flight engineer in history, he told Clara—and so he had studied hard and made the Dean's honor list every year.

In the Dean's office, he stated his case.

"And so you see, sir," he finished, "I helped the Wrights the first time they flew, and they need my help now. I would like to be excused from classes for the next week."

The Dean smiled.

"Mr. Blair, my job is to turn out good engineers, and if the world's first flying machine engineer is a graduate of North Carolina, that will be an honor. I have read all about the Wright brothers, and I am sure you will learn more practical field work in a week with them than you could ever learn here in a week of classes. Just be sure you get back in time to prepare for your final examinations."

Jimmy took the train for home that night.

CHAPTER FOURTEEN

Jimmy Flies at Last

JIMMY drove down the familiar sandy road from Nag's Head to Kill Devil Hill. This time he wasn't driving the buckboard behind old Rock. Instead, he was at the wheel of his father's new automobile. The engine sometimes sputtered and wheezed and threatened to quit, but just the same the auto bounced down the road in a merry style.

Clara sat on the seat beside him. But she was no longer the long-legged little tomboy with flaring red hair who helped her brother fly kites. Instead, she was a prim young school teacher—at least she was going to be next year when she graduated from normal school—and her bright red hair was hidden under a wide-brimmed straw hat tied down by a flowing veil. Her hands were politely folded in her lap, but her brown eyes were shining.

"Jim," she said, "I'm excited."

"You're not half as excited as I am, honey."

"Do you reckon the Wrights have changed?"

"Not if I know old Will and Orv."

"Do you suppose they'll recognize me?"

"Well, now." Jimmy grinned. "Let's wait and see."

The shack near Kill Devil Hill stood just where it had been nearly five years ago, and it was obvious that somebody had come down ahead of time to put it into shape.

Jimmy pulled up in front of it and cut the motor. He got down and was in the act of handing Clara to the ground when Will and Orv came bursting out of its shadowy interior. They were the same old Orv and Will, Jim thought, still half genius and half boy.

"Jim!" Orv slapped him on the shoulder and reached for his hand. "Boy, what have you done to yourself? You're as big as the side of a house!" Then Will was on him, and he was pumping both their hands.

The brothers backed off and looked at him, as though trying to make up their minds about him.

"What's this I hear about Walter Camp saying you were the best halfback in the South?" Orv said.

"Camp must not have seen many halfbacks," Will said, laughing. "This boy's not a football player. He's a flyer. Right, Jim?"

"That's for sure, Will," Jimmy said. "Anybody can play football."

"Just the same," Orv insisted, "the paper said you made the touchdown that beat Army. You can't get out of that."

"Shucks," Jim said. "They just handed me the ball and shoved me toward the goal-line."

In the midst of this banter, Will saw Clara still sitting in the auto.

"You don't say!" he gasped, half in fun. "You can't mean it! This isn't the little redheaded girl who sewed our flying machine wings!"

"Clara!" Orv cried. "You're all grown up! Here, let me help you down."

"You see, Jim," Clara said as Orv handed her out of the high front seat, "I told you they wouldn't know me."

"Don't you think so for a minute, young woman!" Orv laughed. "We'd have known that head of red hair anywhere."

"But now come on inside," Will insisted, "and we'll have a bottle of pop while we talk. I even think we've got some ice to cool it with."

When they were seated around the table inside

the shack, the conversation quieted down and became serious.

"You remember, Jim," Will began, "the last time I saw you, that night we had supper at your house, I said that our big problem was to make flying machines practical? Well, our big chance to prove that they are has finally come. Nobody except Orv and me has ever built a practical flying machine. And if we get this Army contract, we'll have the jump on the whole world. If the Army buys one, it's bound to want more. So will other people. That means we're going to be in business at last."

"We'll build the machines," Orv cut in, "and we'll teach people to fly 'em. In fact, the Army contract says that we have to instruct at least two military flyers."

"I'm going to be one of the first persons you teach," Jimmy said flatly.

"You are, for sure, Jim." Wilbur smiled.

"Now the point is," Will went on, "our machine has to carry a passenger to pass the Army tests. That means we've had to put in seats, and re-rig the controls so the pilot can fly it sitting up instead of lying down. We've got the machine— we shipped it down here, and it arrived yesterday —but we've never tried it with a passenger. If anything goes wrong on the first test, we don't want the public at large to know about it till we've had time to make changes. That's why we came all the way back here to Kitty Hawk."

"When do you perform for the Army?"

"Sometime in September, at Fort Myer, Virginia. But when we make the test there, we want to be sure beforehand that everything is going to be okay."

"Where's the flying machine now, Will?" Jimmy asked curiously, looking around the empty shack.

"She's over on the other side of the hill," Will replied. "Charley Furnas is out there with her."

"We've got a long track that lets her take off on the level ground after we get up speed," Orv explained.

"Can we see her?" Jimmy asked.

"Sure," Will said. "Let's go."

As they were leaving the shack, Jimmy said to Will:

"About this passenger, Will. If you fly the machine, it oughtn't to be Orv. And if Orv flies her, it oughtn't to be you. So—how about me?"

"We figured you'd want to do it, Jim. That's why we asked you to come down."

A short, wiry man, older than either Will or

Orv, was walking around the machine, tinkering with it.

"Jim, this is Charley Furnas," Will said. "You've heard us talk about him. He came down from Dayton to help us out as a mechanic."

Jimmy shook hands absently. He had eyes only for the new *Flyer*. It was a great deal heavier than the 1903 machine. It had a longer wingspread and looked stronger and sturdier. The runners underneath were wider apart and there was now a wheel between them. But in general the lines of the *Flyer* were much the same as those of the original model.

Two small bucket-type seats had been rigged up on the leading edge of the lower wing, and a footrest jutted out in front of them. Two control sticks stuck up on either side of the pilot. With one hand he controlled the warping of the wings, with the other the movable rudders.

"What's that thing?" Jimmy asked, indicating a tall, wooden structure that was built like an oil derrick.

"That's the launching tower," Will explained. "We drop a sixteen-hundred pound weight from the top, and as it falls it pulls a tow-rope that jerks the *Flyer* into the air. That way, we don't need a hill or a heavy wind."

"Is she all set, Charley?" Orv asked.

"She's rarin' to go, Mr. Wright," the mechanic replied.

"Okay, Jim," Orv said. "I'll show you how slick she works."

He climbed into the pilot's seat and pulled his cap down tight on his head. He tested the control sticks, and then Will started the engine. When the propellers were spinning at full speed, with the engine belching smoke and spitting fire, he gave Charley Furnas a signal. The mechanic triggered the launching device, and the falling weight jerked the *Flyer* smoothly along the rail and into the air.

It went up on a steady incline, climbing as it flew, and was soon only a dot in the distance. Then Orv circled her around in a wide arc and came back, passing more than a hundred feet over the heads of the little group below.

Jim didn't quite know what he had expected to see, but this seemed incredible. The first flights four years ago had been little more than feeble, faltering hops, with the flying machine struggling to stay in the air for a few seconds and then quickly flopping back to earth.

But *this* was real flying! This was beating the birds at their own game! Orv was swooping and circling as gracefully as any gull that ever flew. And it looked as if he could stay up there forever if he wanted to—or at least until his gasoline gave out.

Jim stared upward, his mouth open, unable to take his eyes off the flying machine. He stole a side glance at Clara. She, too, was staring into the sky.

Her little red mouth hung open, and her eyes were as big and white as saucers. Jim realized that she had been clutching his arm with both hands.

Now Orv had circled again and was once more headed in their direction. This time he was losing altitude, coming in as though he was sliding down an inclined ramp. At last his runners hit the sand, not a hundred feet from where the watchers stood.

Orv climbed out of his seat and walked toward them.

"Well, Jim, what do you think of her?"

"Gosh! Holy cow, Orv!" Jimmy was groping futilely for words to express the thoughts that were racing through his brain. "Reading your letters about making long flights, and then seeing you really do it—well, it's—it's two completely different things!" He shrugged helplessly. "Gee, Orv! I don't know how to say it!"

Orville and Wilbur laughed, and then Orv called to Charley Furnas.

"Fill her up with gas and check the oil level, Charley. Then we'll put her back on the rail."

When the *Flyer* was once more poised for another flight, Orv said quietly:

"Are you ready to try it, Jim?"

Jimmy's heart jumped into his throat and began to pound wildly. He saw Clara's face grow dead white, and she looked at him with a frightened look in her eyes.

Jim forced a smile, which he spread out into a big grin.

"I was wondering if we were going up today, Orv." He hoped that his jumping insides weren't affecting the tone of his voice. "I haven't been able to wait."

"Good," Orv said. "Come on."

Clara clutched at Jimmy's sleeve.

"Oh, Jim! Jimmy! Please, *please* be careful!"

"Orv is the one you had better tell to be careful. He'll be doing the driving. I'm just going along for the ride."

Then, on an impulse, he bent over and kissed her lightly on the forehead.

"Don't worry, honey. Orv won't let anything happen to me."

Will helped him into the seat at Orv's right, next to the engine. Orv got into the other.

"Now, Jim," Will said earnestly, "I heard your sister tell you a moment ago to be careful. And now I'm telling you, too. It's easy to fall out of this thing, so watch your step. Sit well back in the seat, hold your feet firmly against the cross-bar, and hang onto this strut with one hand. Do that, and you'll be as safe as if you were sitting in church. You all set?"

Jimmy nodded. "Yep!"

When Will started up the engine, it set up a terrific din in Jim's ears. As the propellers began to spin faster the awful racket increased. Riding in a flying machine, he thought, was never going to be exactly what you'd call a quiet and restful experience.

Since speech was impossible, Orville touched Jim's arm and nodded, then placed his hand back on the control stick. Jimmy tightened his grip on the strut. Orv nodded again, this time to Charley Furnas, and the mechanic released the catapulting weight.

The sudden forward motion pressed Jimmy back into his seat. A second later, they were twenty feet in the air and going up. The sand dunes under the wing rolled backward like a moving carpet, and kept getting farther and farther away. In a matter of minutes, they were flying at an altitude Jim estimated as about a hundred and fifty feet.

From this grandstand seat in the sky, the whole peninsula spread out before him. To his left he could see the rolling breakers of the Atlantic, and on his right the quiet waters of Albemarle Bay.

Then they were passing over his house! It looked queer and strange, seeing it from up here. Like a child's playhouse. Rock and Fanny were grazing quietly in the little pasture behind the barn, and some washing was hanging out on the line. There was no sign of his mother. He sure wished she had been out in the yard to see this!

Then they passed over the scattered buildings of the little town of Nag's Head, and he could pick out his father's store on the fishing wharf. Now the noise of the flying machine had begun to attract attention, and people were running out of the stores and shops, looking up and pointing.

Orv made a great sweeping circle that took them out over the open Atlantic. As far as Jim could see, the wind was kicking up little whitecaps, and the sunlight bounced off the water like pinpoints of white fire. Away in the distance, a coastal steamer was plowing along, leaving a long trailing spume of white water in its wake.

Orv completed his circle, and in a few minutes the camp flashed underneath their wings. Clara and Will and Charley waved as they passed over. Jim wanted to wave back, but his right hand had a death-grip on the strut, and his left was clutching the side of the seat. He decided he'd better not. But just at that moment, Orv took one hand from the control stick and waved casually. So Jimmy braced himself hard in the seat, unglued his hand from the strut and waved too. Then he quickly grabbed his hold again. Orv looked at him and grinned.

The wind whipped Jimmy's face and stung his eyes, and the roar of the engine hammered in his ears. But he lost all track of time in the sheer ecstacy of being up here in the air, flying like a bird. He remembered his boyhood dreams of riding the wing of a kite; and his flights on the Wrights' old glider. But *this* was the real thing! This was *flying!* This was what he had always wanted!

Then he noticed that the *Flyer* was losing altitude. The dull, brown sand came rushing up to meet them, and Orville glided in smoothly for his landing. The runners skidded along the sand, and the flying machine came to a stop. Orv cut the engine, and it was all over.

Jimmy climbed stiffly out of his seat. Suddenly, his legs seemed too weak to hold him up, and his first step was a stagger. Then he got control of them, and walked toward Clara and Will.

Clara lunged into his arms, and held her red head tightly against his chest.

Looking over her shoulder, he could see Orv and Will grinning like Cheshire cats. Clara stepped back, and Jim could see that her eyes were filled with tears—and pride.

"Well," Orv said, laughing, "it looks like that Army contract is as good as signed, Will."

"It sure does, little brother."

Then Will said to Jimmy:

"Do you like to fly, boy?"

"Do I like to *fly?* Man, don't ask me crazy questions!"

"He likes to fly, Orv."

"That's good," Orv said.

"When did you say you were graduating from that college, Jim?"

"June the third."

"Well, what do you know, Orv? That's the very date we picked to hire somebody for that new job."

"What new job is that?" Jimmy said.

Will backed off and looked at him and grinned.

"Chief Engineer of the Wright Flying Machine Company," he said.

About the Author

FELIX SUTTON was born in Clarksburg, West Virginia, where he went to school and later graduated from the University of West Virginia, College of Journalism. A former newspaper reporter, sports writer and editor, he has contributed numerous short stories to national magazines both here and in England. In addition to about a dozen adventure stories—largely about the Old West and early American history—he has written several novels for young people. In the early '30's, he barnstormed through the South helping to put on air shows. He and Mrs. Sutton and their three children now live in Connecticut, where he likes to go hunting and fishing—when he can find the time.

About the Artist

LASZLO MATULAY was born in Vienna, Austria, of Hungarian parents. He attended Normal School and studied art in Vienna for five years at the Academy of Applied Arts. In 1935 he immigrated to the U. S. Here, his illustrations have appeared in Harpers Bazaar, Esquire, Mademoiselle, etc., as well as in many books. He has also done commercial art, layouts, and designs for agencies, and has worked as art director in promotions and publications. His prints were exhibited at the World's Fair in 1939, and in the Public Library. He spent three years in the U. S. Army in the European theater of operation in the Second World War. He is married and has two children.

About the Historical Consultant

GROVER LOENING met Wilbur Wright in 1909, in New York, when the first Wright flight was made there. Mr. Loening was then at Columbia University working for the first Degree in Aeronautics in America, which was awarded to him in 1910. Meanwhile, the Wright brothers gave him much technical and engineering instruction, and in 1912 Mr. Loening became the first Chief Engineer of the Wright Company. Mr. Loening continued his career in aviation through the ensuing fifty years, his most notable development having been the first successful amphibian plane. He is active today as a Consultant and Director of several aircraft enterprises and has been awarded the highest honors.